Love is
a time of enchantment:
in it all days are fair and all fields
green. Youth is blest by it,
old age made benign:
the eyes of love see
roses blooming in December,
and sunshine through rain. Verily
is the time of true-love
a time of enchantment — and
Oh! how eager is woman
to be bewitched!

SNOWFLAME

He comes intending to buy her house, never expecting to meet her or to intrude upon her grief the day after her husband's funeral. Drawn to Bruce McClure as if by fate, Elaine Jeffrey welcomes his companionship during a freak winter storm . . . and haltingly confides the anguishing fear that she could have prevented her husband's death. It's sweet relief to find comfort in Bruce's arms, to feel their passion surge into love — but Elaine must confront a sinister truth . . .

CHRISTA MERLIN

SNOWFLAME

Complete and Unabridged

ULVERSCROFT
Leicester

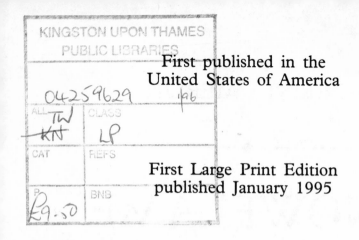
First published in the
United States of America

First Large Print Edition
published January 1995

British Library CIP Data

Merlin, Christa
Snowflame.—Large print ed.—
Ulverscroft large print series: romance
I. Title
823.914 [F]

ISBN 0–7089–3224–X

Published by
F. A. Thorpe (Publishing) Ltd.
Anstey, Leicestershire
Set by Words & Graphics Ltd.
Anstey, Leicestershire
Printed and bound in Great Britain by
T. J. Press (Padstow) Ltd., Padstow, Cornwall

This book is printed on acid-free paper

1

AT noon, snow had begun falling on the rough peaks and narrow valleys of the southern Appalachian mountains. A pewter-colored November sky promised more snow later. But Bruce McClure, maneuvering his four-wheel-drive station wagon up a steep mountain road, noted the signs and then ignored them.

On leave from his legal practice in Atlanta, Bruce had been staying at a local hunt club for over a month, and both his tousled black hair and curling beard were in dire need of a trim. The luxurious shagginess, coupled with a heavy red-and-black-plaid wool shirt, tough jeans, and laced boots, made McClure look more like the son of a mountaineer he had been born than the successful urban attorney he had become. Thirty-five, fit and healthy, his big, muscular body radiated an air of strength, confidence, and maturity; today, his strong-featured face and deep brown eyes wore a look of pleased anticipation.

There was a reason for the look. For years, Bruce had been dreaming of having a home in this rugged country, and this morning, out of the blue, a golden opportunity had fallen into his lap. At least, it sounded like it. If the place was even close to the description, Bruce was sure he'd buy it.

Paul Somers, of the Eagle Real Estate Company, had called early this morning, bursting into speech as soon as Bruce picked up the phone.

"You owe me a dinner for calling you first on this one," Paul had said. "It's Frank Jeffrey's place, and you'll never see a bargain like it again. Only six months old, worth a quarter-million, and Elaine Jeffrey — she's Frank's widow — has set a price of only a hundred fifty thousand. I argued, but she won't listen. Says she wants cash and a quick sale. Meet me there at one o'clock with a pen in your hand for signing the contract. One look will convince you, pal. The damned place has everything."

Bruce had been inclined to believe

Paul. He had heard enough about Jeffrey's magnificent 'hunting lodge' from mutual friends who had visited it. He himself had never seen it. He had barely known Jeffrey, though on occasion they had hunted in the same group. Frank Jeffrey had been known for his cool skill in the field, which had made his recent fatal accident even more shocking to the men who knew him. Seasoned hunters did not, ordinarily, leave their guns cocked and loaded while climbing through a barbed-wire fence. But according to the inquest, the evidence was clear. The trigger of Jeffrey's gun had caught in the wire and discharged a load into his chest, killing him instantly. Thinking of it now as he approached Jeffrey's drive, Bruce shook his head. It showed what could happen in a moment of excitement.

The wind was rising. Snow swirled around the arrangement of rustic logs that marked the entrance to Jeffrey's mountain retreat. Bruce slowed, looking upward at the steep slant of the driveway, noticing that the gravel was covered by a pristine white blanket unmarked by wheels. Either Paul had arrived before it started snowing or he was late. He'd be there, though. Somers wouldn't miss a commission on this.

Going on, winding up through a sprinkle of dark pines, Bruce caught glimpses of the massive lodge through other, winter-bare trees, glimpses that he knew wouldn't show in the summer when the trees were an impenetrable wall of lush green. The house excited him. Built with a foundation of native stone and walls of rough-cut cedar stained a woodsy brown, it stretched along a wide, natural plateau. Protected on the northwest by the rise of the mountain, it overlooked a valley far below. It was two stories high, yet so broad one hardly noticed the extra height. Wheeling into the parking space, Bruce laughed wryly. The place was huge, much too big for a bachelor, yet it was exactly what he wanted.

He could see a car in the open double garage. A small economy model that couldn't belong to Jeffrey. So Paul was there, checking around inside. Bruce went, parking in the other side of the garage, out of the snow. Getting out,

4

grabbing a mackinaw from the back seat as he felt the bite of the icy air, Bruce grinned. He could see a plume of smoke drifting overhead. Paul was setting the scene — the house would be shown to its best advantage, including the cheerful warmth of a fireplace.

Shrugging into his coat, he started around to the front door, glancing at the strong lines of the house with pleasure. Hell, he'd buy it even without a peek inside. It was the house of his dreams. He was still grinning when he thumped the door with his fist, a wide grin that faded fast when the door opened.

It was just not the way to meet a beautiful woman. Not the day after her husband's funeral, and certainly not with the intention of buying her husband's home at half its value. Suddenly, Bruce felt like ghoul, robbing a corpse in front of the grieving family. Fury at Paul Somers for not warning him of her presence flooded his mind along with his own guilt. He hesitated, on the verge of begging her pardon and leaving, but then there was something — something about her that drove straight to his heart

5

and held him there. He stared at her, at the heavy mass of mahogany hair piled untidily on top of her head, at the wide, light gray eyes, black-fringed and impractically large in a small, pale face, and wondered what in God's name the something was.

Elaine Jeffrey stared back at him, a faint tinge of color coming up in her smooth ivory cheeks. She wore a loose, pale green cotton-knit pullover and a pair of light slacks, and was obviously dressed for the warmth of the house, not for the cold blast of wind coming in the open door, nor the snow that now dusted the thick black hair and wide shoulders in front of her. She shivered and wrapped slim arms around herself.

"I suppose," she said tartly, "that you're Bruce McClure. Why don't you come in?"

"I don't want to intrude," Bruce said awkwardly. "I didn't know you were here. I mean, I expected Paul Somers."

"You aren't intruding," Elaine said, and stepped back, putting her hand on the door. "I was expecting you. Come in, please. That air is freezing."

Hastily, Bruce shook himself and stomped his boots, dislodging most of the snow, then stepped inside and shut the door for her. "Sorry," he mumbled, "I wasn't thinking." Now, that was the truth. He hadn't had a coherent thought since the door opened. Only feelings. Feelings that ranged from guilt to pity to a damned inappropriate desire. She really was beautiful. But fragile-looking. Blue smudges around those amazing eyes, faint hollows below her delicate cheekbones. Grief, he supposed, and was again ashamed of his purpose here. Hell, he'd been exulting, even gloating, over the chance of acquiring this house.

"Hang your coat on the rack there," Elaine said calmly, "and come in by the fire. Paul Somers has just called to say he'll be late." Looking at the huge, shaggy man, her gray eyes lost some of their bleakness; a faint warmth shone in their depths before she turned to lead Bruce into the living room.

He followed, leaving the impressive foyer paved with a mosaic of smooth river stones, entering the even more impressive great room, where a fire roared at one end; at the other end was a wall of windows and sliding-glass doors that opened onto a view of a valley and the dim shapes of mountains in the distance. The fire, the view, and even the high cathedral ceiling were all lost on Bruce, whose gaze remained on the woman. His attention had been captured by the incredible delicacy of a small ear and slim neck, a slender shoulder revealed by the wide boat neckline of the pale green knit. A ribbon of rich mahogany hair had escaped the careless knot and lay curled along the neck and shoulder, emphasizing the creamy smoothness of her skin. His eyes, traveling their own path down her narrow, subtly curved figure, past the loose blouse that barely touched the slight flare of hips, came to an abrupt halt at a pair of bare feet. This was not the type of woman he could visualize as Jeffrey's wife. That woman would have been dressed fashionably and been very sophisticated. When this one went to the center of the big room, folded her slender legs, and sat flat on the floor beside a huge pile of scattered papers, a wild hope sprang into his mind. Perhaps she wasn't Frank's widow. Maybe a friend of the widow's, helping out . . .

"Make yourself at home," she said, still calmly. "You might like to tour the house on your own. The upstairs is all open for inspection, I believe, and I think there's some kind of a basement." She looked up at him, the gray eyes impassive again, her hands now occupied with a sheaf of papers. "I'm afraid I wouldn't be of much help. Mr. Somers knows more about my husband's house than I do."

Then she *was* Frank's widow. Fighting a surprisingly intense wave of disappointment, Bruce went to the wall of glass and opened a sliding door, his big hand fumbling and awkward. Stepping out on a narrow balcony, he closed the door behind him, perversely glad of the cold air. Gripping the snow-damp railing, he stared unseeingly at the valley below and the mountains in the distance, forcing himself to remember why he was here and who she was.

He felt like a fool. Beautiful women were no rarity in his life, nor, at thirty-five, was he particularly vulnerable. What made this woman so enormously

9

appealing? What had reached out from that pale, closed face and shaken his heart the way a terrier shook a rabbit? Could it be only pity? Those big, silvery eyes had seemed to dare him to be sorry for her. Yet the situation was bitterly tragic. She had just lost a handsome, virile, and wealthy husband in a senseless accident. Inside, she must be devastated.

"Settle down, dammit!" he said half aloud. "She *wants* to sell the house." He stood in the freezing air a moment more, reminding himself of what Paul Somers had said — cash and a quick sale. She must have her reasons for wanting to get rid of it at once. He released the railing, shook himself again, and reentered the big room, giving the small seated figure a quick glance.

"Great view," he said gruffly. "That's a big plus, up here."

"So I've heard," Elaine answered, putting a bit of amused scorn in her voice. "View sells in the mountains." She looked up, and with the lifting of the small, pale face Bruce was caught again, helpless in a rush of feeling he didn't understand. "Perhaps," she continued, "it gives a feeling of power — looking down at the rest of the world." There was a hint of challenge in the last words.

Bruce scarcely heard her. He *saw* her, with that startling clarity that was reserved for the momentous happenings in life. He saw how small she was, how the mass of heavy hair seemed to burden her slim neck, how delicate her wrists were, circled by the loose knit cuffs. But, most of all, he saw past the polite mask to an agony within. It showed in the unconscious tremor of her lips, in the shadows of her eyes and the tension of trembling fingers. At once he had an almost irresistible impulse to drop to his knees on the floor beside her and gather her into his arms like a hurt child. To hold her and let her cry, to exorcise the demons of grief. But even as he recognized the impulse, he was horrified by the sudden flicker of wonder in her eyes. He looked away, knowing she must have seen at least a hint of how he felt. And, he thought sagely, she also must be thinking he was out of his mind. Which he was. He was sure of that.

"Well," he said hoarsely, "I guess I

will look around the rest of the house — if you're sure you don't mind."

Elaine Jeffrey nodded, the wonder still in her eyes, and as he left the room she let out the breath she had been holding in a long sigh, turning reluctantly back to the papers. For a moment there, the stranger's bearded face had held so much warmth and tenderness that Elaine had felt like scrambling to her feet, burrowing against that big body, and crying out all the bitter frustration and the terrible guilt of the past five days. How embarrassed he would have been!

It was strange, she thought, how from the moment she had opened the door she had felt she knew Bruce McClure and that he knew her. When his dark eyes had widened and stared at her, she had almost expected him to call her by name, to tell her where they had met, possibly years ago. Yet she knew that was impossible; she would have remembered him clearly. It was only an illusion. And, right now, it was natural that he might feel sympathy. Paul Somers had told her that Bruce McClure had known Frank and knew how he had died. Perhaps McClure had been one of Frank's friends.

She thought about that and then shook her head. She had only just met Bruce McClure, but friendship between him and Frank seemed unlikely. Her mouth, which had begun to relax, straightened again into a flattened line. A point, she thought, for McClure.

Picking up another sheaf of unpaid bills, she began sifting through them methodically, tossing aside duplicates. For months on end, the same bills . . .

Overhead, her keen ears caught the soft sound of a door closing. Somers had told her that Bruce McClure was a sure bet — he'd buy the house. She hoped so. She raised her head and looked around at the sumptuous room, brightened by the firelight that gave a glow to the fine, leather-covered, down-soft furniture, and deepened the tone of the thick, Persian blue rug. Professionally decorated, the house held no imprint of Frank's personality except for the gun collection housed in a carved, glass-fronted case Elaine knew had cost thousands. But, then, none of the places where Frank had lived had ever been stamped by his identity; he tired of them too quickly and moved on.

She went back to the bills, noting again that many of them were for these furnishings. The best of everything, even in a hunting lodge. Even if it took his last cent. Which it had — these papers proved that. Thank God the house itself was free and clear and the money from the sale would pay his debts. Then, and only then, would she be free of the burden of being Frank Jeffrey's wife.

Getting to her feet, Elaine picked up the pile of duplicates and took them to the fireplace. Kneeling, she began slowly feeding them to the leaping flames, two or three at a time, her face thoughtful.

Had it been only two years since she and Frank had separated? So much had happened since then that it seemed a good deal longer. First, the secretarial course she had paid for herself out of a small inheritance. Then the job, and she'd been able to move from a rented room to a cheerful apartment.

In the weeks just after she had left Frank, Elaine had hoped he'd see reason and allow her a divorce; at the end of the first year, she had reluctantly settled for a legal separation. A little freedom, she had decided, was better than none at all.

Then Frank had insisted on giving her an allowance, but a small one according to his way of thinking — a blatant way of reminding her of the unlimited funds she would have if she came back to him. A paper trail that was supposed to lead her home, the checks arrived promptly on the first of every month, and Elaine had sent them back, just as promptly, on the second. There had never been anything in the envelopes but the checks, until this last one, which had been accompanied by a note.

The note had disturbed her. Even while she hunted up an envelope to return the check, her thoughts had remained fixed on the cryptic message. She had gone over and over it in her mind, and then, picking it up again, she had reread it.

He had written:

Cash it while it's still good. That won't be long. I've lost it all, 'Laine. Every dime. Or should I say I've used it up? Can't complain, though, I've lived the way I wanted. There's a way out, and I'm taking it. You'll be free at last.

It hadn't surprised Elaine that Frank had managed to deplete the immense fortune he had inherited. That had seemed inevitable. But the rest of it kept nagging at her. She wished he had said either less or more. What had he meant by 'a way out'? Frank had never worked, only played. She supposed it was conceivable that one of his wealthy friends might give him an honorary position of some kind, but she couldn't imagine Frank living on a salary, no matter how large. And what did he mean, she'd be free? He had told her from the day she left him that he'd fight any attempt she made to divorce him, that the only thing that would free her would be his death. Her eyes had widened at the thought; her heart had sunk. But Frank wouldn't . . . or would he? Was that his way out?

She had mulled it over for a full day, and then, frightened by her thoughts, she had asked for time off from her job and packed her clothes. She no longer loved Frank, if indeed she ever had truly loved him, but there were those years together and still a true sense of responsibility. She had driven the hundreds of miles between the South Carolinian coast where she lived and worked to these mountains, only to find his house empty. She had checked into a small motel in the town and contacted the county sheriff. The sheriff knew Frank, and he had told her Frank was off on a hunting trip with some of his buddies. There were several places the men might be, none of them accessible by car except for one farm in an adjoining valley. Elaine had gone there, without results, and then back to the motel to wait, full of doubts.

Then, that evening, they had brought his body in and told her about the accident, which had happened on that farm. The rush of guilt she had felt was overpowering. No matter how hard she tried, she couldn't make herself believe it had been an accident, nor could she stop thinking that she could have prevented it. She was sure if she had gone to Frank as soon as the note had come, she could have reasoned with him. He was dead at thirty-eight because she hadn't cared enough.

The papers were gone, but she continued to kneel by the fire, staring at the still-burning logs. A muted sound broke through her thoughts and she glanced up, seeing Bruce McClure coming in from the foyer. He moved quietly for such a big man, smoothly and well coordinated, as if he were comfortable with his size. She got to her feet, thinking with surprise that it was somehow reassuring to have him in the house. Alone in this big place, isolated in the wilds of the mountains, Elaine had felt uncertain. She gave Bruce what she hoped was a cheerful smile.

"Well, did you see all you wanted to see, Mr. McClure?"

"It's even better than I had hoped," Bruce said gruffly. He had seen the shine of tears in her eyes. "There's a full basement, by the way. Warm and dry." He strode past her, avoiding another glance at her face, and stood by the fire. "It's snowing hard, Mrs. Jeffrey. No word from Somers?"

18

As if on cue, the telephone in the foyer rang. Elaine ran to answer it, glancing through a window as she passed. The air was white with snow; she couldn't see past the shrubbery that hugged the house. A storm? There had been no forecast of a storm. Yet the stone mosaic was colder on her bare feet.

"It's Paul Somers," she said, coming back into the living room a few minutes later. He's not able to come up." She saw the bearded face tighten. "He tells me there's a storm, and it's headed this way. He wants to speak to you."

Bruce nodded abruptly and left the room. Standing at the window, watching the swirling flakes, Elaine could hear the deep murmur of his voice as he talked with Somers. Paul had asked her if she was all right, if there were food and fuel in the house. He had said it might be a day or two before she could come down the mountain for provisions. He had sounded excited. From what he implied, there weren't many severe storms in this locality. And, when he discovered that McClure was still there, he had suggested that she ask him to stay.

19

"Bruce is damned handy in an emergency," he had added. "You'll be safe with him."

"I'll be safe anyway," Elaine had replied stiffly. "I have more than enough food and fuel." That was true. The freezer in the kitchen was stocked with an amazing array of food, and the central heat was electric and automatic. Even if the power went off, there was plenty of wood for the fireplace. But would McClure be safe? There would be poor visibility on the steep mountain roads. She had been about to ask Somers what he'd heard of road conditions when he asked to speak to Bruce.

Now, still standing at the window, she heard the click as McClure hung up the phone. She turned to look at him inquiringly as he came in.

"I can't blame Somers," Bruce said grimly. "I guess it is a bad one, and getting worse." He looked at her searchingly, his dark brows knitted. "Will you be all right here alone, Mrs. Jeffrey?"

"Yes, of course." But she wouldn't like it; she knew that. It was bad enough in good weather to be alone in such a remote spot. "What about yourself? It's a long drive down in this kind of weather."

"I'll make it. I've got the right vehicle for it." He hesitated. "Plenty of food? It's liable to last a while."

She laughed for the first time, a throaty ripple of wry amusement that parted the curved lips and showed a glistening of small white teeth. "I could feed a dozen for a week with what's in the freezer. You shouldn't worry about me."

He smiled back at her, a smile that lighted up his bearded face. "But I do . . . a little," he answered, surprising her. "A lot of things can happen in a storm like this. You could lose power as trees go down . . . " He was still hesitating, making no move to get his coat and go. "I could stay," he added, the skin above his beard flushing slightly, "if — if you'd feel more secure."

Elaine felt suddenly breathless. "But — your family," she said. "Won't they be looking for you?"

The brown eyes touched hers, warm and concerned. "I have no family. I've been staying at the hunt club." Watching, he saw a shadowy flicker of doubt in the depths of her huge eyes. "It's a big house," he added gently. "You wouldn't have to know I was here unless you needed me. I . . . wouldn't bother you, Mrs. Jeffrey."

In that moment, Elaine realized how badly she wanted him to stay. A surge of deep, warm relief went through her as she also realized he meant every word he had said. She smiled, completely unconscious of how her face suddenly glowed, her eyes sparkled.

"You won't bother me at all, Mr. McClure. I'd love to have company through the storm, if you're sure you don't mind staying."

Bruce let out his breath, his whole body relaxing, his smile quirking again through the black beard. "Mind? I'd like to stay. But I'd feel better about it if you called me Bruce. It's friendlier."

She laughed, again only a small tipple of sound but this time warm and genuine. "Yes, it is. Call me Elaine, then. And if you'll give me a few moments to shower and dress, I'll raid that freezer for us."

Watching her leave, listening to the soft, light patter of bare feet on the stairs, Bruce blessed the storm. Without it, Somers would have been here, the contract signed, and then he would have had to leave without any real excuse to see Elaine Jeffrey again.

Moving to the fireplace, he put a fresh log on the smoldering coals and stood watching the tiny flames lick up around it. Now he had a chance. He would have to move slowly, but move he would. Behind the pain and uncertainty in those eyes, behind the strange agony, there was still that something. Something lovely, something tender. He couldn't define it, but he knew he needed it. Badly.

2

UPSTAIRS there were four bedrooms, four baths. Elaine had taken the smallest guest room as her own, at one end of the long hall. Now, before she went in to shower, she took fresh sheets, pillowcases, and an extra blanket from the linen closet, then went swiftly to the other end of the hall. Here was the master bedroom, luxurious in muted browns and golds, with an amber rug like thick turf. After stripping the king-sized bed efficiently, she made it up with fresh linen, checked the bath for supplies of towels and soap, shrugged upon glancing at the electric shaving equipment — with that beard? — and then left, leaving the door ajar and dumping the stripped sheets down the laundry chute. She had thought of laying out a pair of Frank's pajamas and a robe, but she doubted that Bruce McClure could get into them. The bottoms, maybe, but never the tops, not over those shoulders and that chest.

Back in her room, she found herself humming in the shower. She stopped, feeling a twinge of guilt, and finished soaping and rinsing in silence. Still, she was very conscious of how much better she felt knowing she wasn't alone, rattling around in this huge house while a storm raged outside. How lucky that Bruce had wanted to stay! She felt absolutely safe with him. Which was strange, she realized, considering they'd just met.

Sometimes one just knew, she thought, getting out of the shower and wrapping a towel around herself without a glance at the mirrored wall. Elaine had ignored her body for some time, content to wash it and feed it and forget it. The fact that her rounded breasts were still high and youthful didn't interest her, nor did the smooth lines of her narrow waist and slender, curved hips. Her body was supple and strong in spite of its size, and it worked well. That was enough.

Still, choosing something to wear, she honored the occasion of having a guest by putting on a more feminine outfit: a silk blouse and skirt, the blouse white and Victorian-looking, the skirt long and a deep forest green. The neckline of the blouse went well with a more skillfully pinned topknot of gleaming hair; the silk skirt moved softly around her slender legs as she came downstairs and entered the living room.

Bruce stood up as she came in, his brown eyes lit by the golden fire as they traveled over her. "Charming," he said. "It suits you." He would have liked to say more. He would have liked to put an arm around her waist and draw her close, breathe in her scent, and touch his lips to that small ear, a thought that made him very conscious of his unkempt beard. "It's early yet," he added, turning away to prevent any of that happening. "Is there a place I can clean up a bit?"

"Of course. I've made up a room for you." Elaine's eyes were warm, resting on him, her lips curved in a smile. He was so big, so solid and dependable-looking. "Up the stairs and to the right, all the way. I'll go defrost something tasty."

In the kitchen, Elaine unbuttoned her cuffs and rolled her sleeves above the elbow, tied a kitchen towel around her waist, and set to work. Some decorator, she had decided, had had a field day here. The kitchen was a wild burst of colors, patterned after the flamboyant Mexican tiles on the floor. Red, orange, and yellow cabinets flared against the white wall; the counter tops were an astringent green, inset with white marble for pastry, and a butcher block for meats. The appliances were sparkling stainless steel, even the huge freezer in one corner. But at least it was cheerful, glowing with color and light against the monochromatic background outside. Nothing could be seen through the windows but driven snow, pushed by a strong wind that howled faintly through the double-paned glass. It was good, she thought, to be safe and warm and cooking dinner for two.

When Bruce came down and made his way to the kitchen, there was a bottle of sparkling Burgundy cooling in a deep clay container, steaks were defrosting in the microwave, and scrubbed Idaho potatoes were waiting to be baked. Elaine was putting a salad together, slicing mushrooms into torn spinach leaves. She looked up and smiled.

"I thought we'd better eat early. If the power goes off, we might end up cooking in an open fireplace."

Bruce laughed. "I can do that, if necessary. But I hope it won't be."

"Me, too." She picked up a crisp piece of fried bacon and came close to him, holding it up. "Here, try this. It's Danish and mild. I thought it might go well in the salad. What do you think?"

He looked down at her, tempted. If it had been any other woman, he would have thought she was being flirtatious. He bit off half of the strip carefully and watched her put the remainder in her own mouth, chewing thoughtfully, still looking at him.

"You trimmed your beard! Too bad. It looked so soft and fluffy, as if you were a young Santa Claus."

"The bacon," Bruce said solemnly, "would be good in the salad. The beard is still soft." He took her wrist and brought her open hand to the side of his face, smiling at her startled look. "See? It only looks bristly." He knew he should go no further, but he couldn't resist the small palm. He turned his head

28

slightly and kissed it before letting it go. "However," he added unevenly, "your hand is softer!"

Elaine was suddenly, blindingly, aware of two things: one, Bruce McClure might not be quite as safe as she'd thought; and two, the pressure of his firm lips on her palm had sent a blazing reminder to a part of her that had been lying dormant, and had started a small but very pleasant fire. She turned away rather awkwardly.

"Then I'll . . . I'll crumble the bacon in," she said, stumbling over words, "while you . . . well, pour the wine, if you will. I imagine the steaks are defrosted, and the potatoes will take only ten minutes or so. I mean, we'll be eating very soon."

He had upset her. He could have kicked himself for that. "It sounds great," he said, falsely jovial, and headed for the wine. He handled the bottle like an expert, gently. The cork came out with only a hollow sigh; the wine bubbled merrily into the glasses. He handed her one.

"I'll fix a table in front of the fire. That dining room across the foyer is too big for two," he said, and escaped from temptation, carrying his own glass with him.

Elaine went on with her cooking, popping the potatoes into the microwave, broiling the steaks. She felt oddly lonely now in the empty kitchen, and when Bruce came back in she looked at him carefully. For the first time, she took note of his extreme masculinity — the heavy muscles of his shoulders and back, the lean strength of his long legs. With his beard close-trimmed, she could follow the line of his strong jaw, the corded power of his neck. The warmth and concern were still in his brown eyes, but he no longer seemed like a young Santa Claus. Kind, yes, and sympathetic. And, as Paul Somers had said, probably damned handy in an emergency. But male. Definitely, dominatingly male. A force to be reckoned with.

Her hands shook a little as she picked up the salad bowls to carry them in. It was funny that at twenty-eight she didn't know how to deal with any man except Frank. She'd been eighteen when they'd married, and it had taken a lot of painful lessons during a number of years to learn how to cope with him. But that knowledge didn't help now. Elaine was too intelligent to think that all men were alike; she instinctively knew that the differences between Frank and Bruce were chasms wide. It was just that the little scene in the kitchen had added an entirely new dimension to Bruce McClure. Nothing unpleasant, just unsettling. Maybe exciting. Walking through to the table set by the fire, she smiled suddenly to herself. It didn't matter. She trusted him. Something deep inside told her she could.

Standing with his back to the blaze, silhouetted by golden light, Bruce was a dark giant. He drained his glass of wine and stepped forward to take the bowls from her. The steaks were still sizzling on their oval, stainless-steel platters, and the odor was seductive.

"I'm starving," he announced, holding Elaine's chair for her. "I may be losing control."

She laughed and sat down quickly, whisking off the kitchen towel she'd used as an apron, rolling down her sleeves, then fastening the ruffled cuffs. Bruce sat down opposite her and reached for the wine to refill their glasses.

"I'm hungry, too," she said absently, fascinated by the skill of his big hand, expertly pouring the sparkling ruby wine into the fragile glasses. From the size of him she'd expected some blundering, yet he was anything but awkward. He was as deft, she thought, as any sophisticated city man . . . She stopped the thought, amazed at herself, and took the glass he held out to her. Paul Somers had told her Bruce was a highly successful attorney in Atlanta! What was she thinking of?

"I keep forgetting you're civilized," she said without thought. "I guess it's the clothes and the beard."

Bruce burst out in deep, surprised laughter. "You may be closer to the true me than you think. I was raised in these mountains, and when I come back to them I revert rapidly. I feel a lot more at home in these jeans and boots than I do in a three-piece suit."

Now she was fascinated by his laugh. Not just by the rich, deep sound, but by the strong white teeth and the shape of his mouth. She looked away with an effort and applied herself to her dinner. "I prefer casual clothes myself," she said after a moment. "When I get home from work, the first thing I do is change to jeans and take off my shoes."

"You work?"

Elaine looked up, meeting his astounded gaze. "Yes." There was no reason now to shield Frank's pride. "I'm a secretary in a small town in South Carolina."

"But . . . why?" His gaze went involuntarily to the luxury surrounding them. "Surely you don't need to."

"I've been legally separated from Frank for over two years," Elaine said steadily. "And I prefer to support myself."

His eyes came back to her, still surprised, but with another quality that seemed to mix admiration with relief. "Then why are you here?" he asked gently. "Why not let others take on the chore of settling his affairs?"

Elaine couldn't bring herself to mention Frank's note. Even the thought of it brought to the fore the searing guilt she was trying to forget. She took a sip of wine and managed an evasive answer that was nevertheless true. "It seems to be up to me. Alfred Fenton, Frank's lawyer, told me after the funeral that I'm named as executrix of his estate."

Bruce was sorry he'd asked. The small face again wore the polite mask that shut him out. He knew Fenton, a close crony of Jeffrey's who had been on the hunting trip — had, in fact, found the body. Well, Fenton had a reasonably good reputation in legal circles; he'd probably be all the help she'd need. Bruce nodded and began talking of other things. Light, impersonal things.

Gradually, Elaine relaxed. Her smile came and went; she laughed occasionally, that small ripple of sound he listened for. They carried the dishes to the kitchen and stacked them in the dishwasher together. Bringing out brandy to serve with the coffee, Elaine glanced at the wall of glass and saw nothing but a dark, crystalline veil with tiny points of light reflected from sleet. She repressed a shudder. "I wish it would stop."

"I'm afraid it's settled in. Hard to guess how long it will last." As they sat down in their chairs again, Bruce raised his glass to her in a half salute. "I'm lucky to be here with such pleasant company. There will be a bunch of irritable, discontented men at the hunt club."

Elaine laughed, kicking off her shoes and settling back with her feet tucked up under the dark green skirt. "I feel lucky, too," she said, sipping the brandy, feeling the warmth of it spreading a rosy glow inside her. "This would have been awful, alone." Her heavy hair was, as always, beginning to slip. Setting her glass on the table beside her, she sat up and took out the pins, putting them in her lap as the shining red-brown mass fell and covered her shoulders and back. With the ease of practice, she scooped it all back from her face with both hands and began to pin it up again.

Watching her, Bruce was jolted by desire. The line of her slim, upraised arms was so graceful; the silk blouse drew tight and outlined her high, rounded breasts. Her face was lit by the glow of the fire, her expression serious as she concentrated on the placement of the pins. Bruce ached to reach over and pull her into his lap, take the pins out again, and bury his hands in that silky hair while he kissed her. For one wild moment, he was tempted to try it. She might not object too strenuously — he had sensed her response when he'd kissed her palm . . .

He moved restlessly in his chair, angry with himself. Maybe she wasn't mourning her husband after being separated that long, but something was tearing her up inside. She didn't need some unfeeling clod putting pressure on her. Besides, he'd said he wouldn't bother her. Dragging her into his lap would bother the hell out of her, to say nothing of the other things that would occur to him once he had her in his arms.

"There," Elaine said, settling back again and picking up her glass. "Maybe it'll hold until bedtime."

Bruce immediately visualized her in a filmy nightgown, her hair loose and shining. He felt his body react predictably and tore his imagination away from that picture. Leaning forward, he cradled his glass in both hand and stared at the fire. "Why not leave it down? It's beautiful."

"That's for kids," Elaine said, yawning. "I'm twenty-eight." She glanced at him, smiling. "I should have it cut, I suppose."

"You wouldn't!"

She laughed. "Men! What is it with you about long hair? Some atavistic memory of it being a convenient handle for dragging women around?"

Bruce leaned back, chuckling, glad of her suddenly light teasing. Better than the long thoughts she'd seemed to be having.

"Maybe. I imagine it really was convenient. Preferable to dragging them by an arm and possibly dislocating a shoulder. Who would stir the pot?"

Elaine dissolved in giggles. "I was right. You aren't civilized. The man could stir the pot."

"He was too busy," Bruce said judiciously. "He had to guard the cave against all the ferocious animals."

"And storms?" she asked softly. "That's what you're doing, isn't it? Guarding the cave, the safe place . . . "

He looked at her, snuggled back in the deep, soft chair, her face turned toward him, her eyes shining, warm and trustful.

I'm falling in love with her, he thought incredulously, and stood up. He couldn't stay here in this room, not now, now without touching her.

"You've reminded me of my duties," he said, making himself smile. "I'd better take a look. Is there a door leading into the garage?"

Elaine nodded and sat up. "On the far side of the kitchen. I'll show you."

"I'll find it," he said abruptly, and turned away.

"Wait!" She scrambled to her feet and ran to the foyer for his mackinaw, brought it back, and helped him into it. "One of your duties is to *not* get pneumonia," she said, reaching to pull up the hood. "Remember that." Her smiling mouth was close enough to kiss. And it looked very kissable.

"I'll try," he said gruffly, wondering if she knew what she was doing to him. If he could be sure she was issuing a playful invitation, he'd have her in bed before she found out what was happening. But, dammit! he *wasn't* sure. Maybe it was wishful thinking — he'd been doing plenty of that.

Stepping into the garage, he was glad of the shock of cold air. He turned on the light, looking at the small car that must be hers; at his heavy wagon with its big snow tires. The door of the garage was open, and the wind had piled drifts against the rear of the cars. He looked for a shovel, found one in a storage room, then bent to the work with a will, glad to have something to do. When he'd cleared most of it, he found the garage button and lowered the door, shutting out the snow and wind. The door held solidly against the buffeting. A good door. A good house. He still wanted it, but there was a mysterious woman inside he wanted more. He'd gotten to the point of wondering if she'd be happy living in the house her husband had built. He took the shovel back and hung it up, coming out of the storage room to find Elaine shivering in the open doorway, looking for him.

"You'll freeze," he warned, hastily bundling her back in, following, then shutting the door behind him. His breath had frosted on his beard; he rubbed the iciness away with a rough hand. "If you're going sightseeing, wear a coat."

"I was worried," she said, rubbing her arms. "I didn't think you'd be so long. Is it bad?"

"Pretty deep. They'll be a while digging us out of this." He grimaced, shouldering out of the mackinaw. "I'm supposed to try a case in Atlanta on Wednesday. I doubt I'll make it."

"That long?"

He nodded. "I expect so. They'll dig the town out first." In command of himself now, he put an arm around her shoulders and led her toward the living room. "Let's get to the fire. It's more cheerful. And don't worry. We're lucky to be where we are."

Elaine's heart sank. Her employer had grumbled enough about a five-day absence; now it looked like ten. Three before she could even meet with Mr. Fenton and get started.

"I'll lose my job," she mourned, sitting down on the edge of her chair, "and it's a good one."

"The next one will be better," Bruce

said, sinking deep in the other chair.

"Easy to say."

She had said it lightly, but he could see the real worry in her eyes. "Easy to mean," he said gently. "You'll be paid well for taking care of Jeffrey's estate. Fees for an executrix of an extensive estate run high."

Elaine leaned back, making a sound somewhere between a laugh and a groan. "Not this time. There's no money."

His dark brows shot up. "*No* money?"

"None."

He took that in, his surprise fading as he remembered talk of Jeffrey's extravagances. "There's the house," he said finally. "And maybe other assets you don't know about."

"No other assets," she said firmly, "and the price of the house will just take care of his debts."

"Well, for godsake," Bruce burst out, "set the price higher. You're way under market, you know. At least save a *little* for yourself."

"No," Elaine said quietly. "I set that price because it matched the amount of his debts." She looked at Bruce, wondering what he would think if she told him she couldn't bear to profit from a death that she could have prevented if she'd tried. She thought he might understand, at that. But Frank must have had a reason to disguise his suicide; she'd keep his secret if she could. He probably hadn't wanted anyone to know he was that desperate. "I still prefer to support myself," she added, and stood up, pale and withdrawn. "I think I'm tired. If you'll excuse me, I'll go to bed."

"Of course." Bruce rose, his dark eyes mirroring concern. "I hope I haven't upset you."

"You haven't." She reached out to him involuntarily, her hand resting for a moment on his arm, her gray eyes warm again. "Just the opposite, Bruce. You made it a very nice evening. Goodnight."

"Goodnight." When she left, Bruce sat down again to wait for the dying of the fire. He wasn't in the least tired or sleepy. He was charged with energy, aching with a need to go out and fight dragons. But whatever beast was gnawing at Elaine was hidden and obscure. Before he could fight it, he had to get it out in the open. And, dammit, he would! His office in Atlanta would have to get along without him until this was settled.

3

THE telephone rang shortly after dawn. Hastily wrapping herself in a fleecy blue robe, Elaine ran to the extension in the upper hall.

"Mrs. Jeffrey? It's a relief to hear your voice. We've been worried about you." The voice was faint and there was a thrumming on the line, but still she recognized Alfred Fenton's high-pitched tone.

"It's Mr. Fenton, isn't it? I think the storm has damaged the lines."

He was talking again, the sound fading and then coming back, stronger and clearer. "Beth was just saying if we'd had warning of this weather, we could have brought you here to our house. Are you all right?"

Glancing up, Elaine saw the door of the master bedroom swing open. Bruce had pulled on his jeans, but that was all. Seeing her already at the phone, he stepped back and shut the door, leaving her with an impression of a bare, massive chest centered by a patch of wiry black curls, a pair of thick, wide shoulders, and a lot of muscles that flexed and gleamed.

"I'm fine," she said faintly, and looked down at herself, at the gaping robe and the cleavage it revealed. "Please don't worry about me. I'm not in any danger here." She pushed back her hair nervously, wondering if that was quite true.

There was a confused sound of voices, and then Fenton came back, strongly. "Write down this number," he was saying, "so you can call if you have an emergency." He gave her the number and she tried to memorize it. Was there ever a pen near a phone? "That's the mountain patrol," Fenton added. "They'll make it through if you need them. Beth and I hate you being up there alone."

He sounded, Elaine thought, overly solicitous. As if he were trying to make an impression. Anyway, the number of the mountain patrol was listed prominently in the front of the phone book. "I'm not . . . " she began, and then hesitated, wondering if she should mention Bruce. It would take a lot of explanation. " . . . not having any trouble at all. But thank you for your concern."

It wasn't any of Fenton's business whether she was alone or not. She scarcely knew the man, having seen him only at the inquest and at the funeral. He had taken her aside once the funeral was over and told her she'd have to stay on, that she was Frank's choice as executrix, and that he, as Frank's lawyer, would do everything he could to help her. He was a lanky man with a habit of bending over people shorter than he was, which had made her feel trapped. He had smiled pleasantly, but his eyes had been wary. He'd explained that his wife would have been there, but she was too much upset by it all. 'A bitter thing,' he had added, 'an accident like that. Of course, you'll meet her later. You'll like Beth.'

Elaine jerked her mind back to the present and tried to make out what he was saying. She had already missed part of it.

" . . . will be clear in a day or so. Then Beth and I would like to have you as a

46

houseguest. It will be more convenient for us both, Elaine, while we go over the estate."

"I believe we have a bad connection," Elaine said hastily. "I'm only getting part of what you're saying. I'll call you when the weather clears."

"Oh. Well, all right. I'll be waiting for your call."

After hanging up, Elaine fled to her room. Fenton could have waited until a decent hour to call, and Bruce wouldn't have seen her with her hair wild and tangled, her robe open almost to her waist. She glanced through the windows as she headed for the bath. She saw that the wind had abated a little, but the snow was still falling thickly. Another day, at least. She pushed down the tiny tremor of excitement at the thought of being snowbound with Bruce that much longer, and advised herself not to be juvenile. By now, he might be regretting his decision to stay. Missing that case in court tomorrow would bother him.

She took her time, washing her hair, blowing it dry, weaving it into a thick braid to hang down her back. Dressed in old, faded jeans and a blue velour pullover, she hunted out a pair of après-ski socks, wildly colored, heavy knit affairs with sewn-on leather soles.

Halfway down the stairs, she caught the welcome odor of brewing coffee and frying bacon. Following her nose, she went into the kitchen and stopped abruptly, trying not to laugh.

"Good morning. You don't look very comfortable."

Turning from the stove, Bruce grinned at her. "Best I could do with a limited wardrobe. I washed my clothes and they're in the dryer." He was wearing a scarlet silk robe that was strained to the bursting point across his shoulders, its sleeves halfway up his thick forearms. It left most of his chest bare but lapped at the waist and covered him decently to his knees. "Want your eggs scrambled?"

Elaine nodded, suddenly shy in the presence of so much bare masculinity, and began to set the kitchen table with places for two. Bruce looked as if he had just stepped from the shower, his tumbled black hair and beard still damp, his skin glowing. When she stood near

48

him pouring coffee into the mugs he'd set out, she caught a scent of soap and musky maleness that set her pulse throbbing. She could feel it pounding in her throat and had the uncomfortable feeling that if he looked he could see it.

"That was Mr. Fenton on the phone," she said to break the silence. "I guess they were wondering if I was all right."

"Al? How well do you know him?"

She put the mugs on the table and sat down as he brought over the platter of bacon and eggs. "Not well at all. What can you tell me about him?"

Dropping into his chair, Bruce frowned thoughtfully. "Not much, really. I guess he has a pretty good practice, but, then, he had a pretty good start. He married into Harrison and Toth, one of the biggest of Atlanta's legal firms." He glanced at Elaine and smiled. "Not to put Al down — he's worked hard, in spite of a rich wife. Beth was a Harrison."

"A point in his favor," Elaine said slowly. It surprised her. Fenton hadn't seemed a strong character, more a puzzling mixture of officiousness and false charm. "What's she like?"

Eating hungrily, Bruce shrugged. "Pretty. Rather spoiled, I think. Likes a lot of attention." He pushed the platter toward Elaine. "Eat. Put some roses in those cheeks."

Startled, Elaine laughed at the old-fashioned phrase and then helped herself to generous portions. "You sound like my grandfather." She looked up and caught his eyes on her in a very ungrandfatherly expression. "Well," she said, hastily returning to the former conversation, "Fenton wants to get together with me as soon as possible to settle the estate."

"He should be a help," Bruce said gently. "That's more or less his specialty — estates." Having looked at her fully, he could hardly tear his eyes away. The sweptback, gleaming hair accentuated the fine bones of her face, the creamy smoothness of her skin. She looked, he thought, as fresh and appealing as an opening flower. "You look as if you slept well," he added carefully.

"Well, yes, I did." Faint color rose in her cheeks. She hadn't slept at all until she had heard his footsteps on the stairs, heard the slight hesitation at the top and then the gradually receding sound as he went down the hall. There had been that split-second of wondering if he'd turn toward her room, and afterward a moment of considering what she would have done if he did. Now, seated across from him in this thoroughly domestic scene, she was suddenly engulfed by a fantasy of herself naked in his arms, curled against that broad chest. It shook her to her toes. Her breath caught in her throat, her heart pounded idiotically, and a lazy, insistent curl of heat stirred and spread seductively in her depths. Shocked and weak, she transfered her gaze to her plate and began to eat. That was ridiculous. It was neither the time nor the place for her long-subdued sexuality to reassert itself. "I hope you found your room comfortable," she added belatedly.

"Very comfortable," he said huskily, as if he read her thoughts.

"Good." She kept her eyes on her plate.

They finished the meal in a charged silence. Then Elaine shooed him from the kitchen to dress while she cleared up the dishes.

It was as she shut the dishwasher and switched it on that the thought came to her that she was no longer a married woman. A simple, obvious fact, but in the traumatic aftermath of Frank's death, it hadn't occurred to her until now. For the past two years, she had refused so many advances on the grounds that she was married that now it was a deeply ingrained habit to consider herself off limits to any interested man. The friends she had made since she left Frank had thought she was crazy. A favorite remark had been: 'You don't think *he's* doing without, do you?'

She had known he wasn't. Frank had never confined himself to one woman, not even the first year they'd been married. He had been unashamedly promiscuous and had thought his young wife's objections absurd. 'I *married* you,' he had explained patiently. 'You're my wife, 'Laine. The others are only recreation. Don't you see the difference?'

She'd been full of ideals, and she thought he would change once she had made herself into exactly what he wanted. By the time she gave up trying, her once warm and joyous sensuality had been completely numbed by the feeling that she was part of a harem.

Maybe, she thought now, she had used her married state as an excuse those two years. With no desire of her own, it had been easy to say no. But if Bruce followed through on some of those looks he'd been giving her . . . what, then? She was no longer numb, obviously, and she was free.

You'll be free at last. The words from Frank's note came back to her like a blow, followed immediately by the sickening sense of guilt. She bit her lip and moved, walking restlessly to the window. She had to get over that; somehow she had to forget it. She'd made a mistake and Frank had died, but there was nothing she could do about it now.

The hum of the dishwasher covered the sound of Bruce's footsteps. Dressed in the laundered jeans and heavy plaid shirt, he stopped in the doorway and looked at her, realizing she was caught again in the sadness he didn't understand. With her head bowed, her forehead pressed against the glass, and her slim hands shoved deep inside the pockets of her jeans, she looked young and defenseless, lost in sorrow. His heart twisted with the desire to comfort her. Moving quietly, he crossed the space between them and grasped the thick braid of silky hair, giving it a gentle tug.

"It can't be that bad, love."

Startled, Elaine turned and found herself inches from his warm bulk, the hand holding her braid still behind her, his arm half around her. Looking up, she met his brown eyes, and the look in them melted her last ounce of reserve. She leaned forward, burrowing into the hollow of his shoulder, wrapping her arms around his waist, feeling his arms surround her tightly, one hand cradling the back of her head.

She cried, making very little fuss about it, swallowing sobs, her chest heaving with the effort of holding them back. But she couldn't hold back the words.

"I was such a *coward*, Bruce . . . I could have st-stopped him if I'd tried . . . but I was so a-afraid of getting involved with him again." She cried harder, tightening her arms desperately. "I'm so ashamed . . . so ashamed . . ."

Holding her, feeling the trusting small figure clinging to him with surprising strength, Bruce was cautious about making any sudden moves. What she was saying made no sense to him, but he waited, stroking her slender back gently until she was through crying. Then, as she turned and fumbled for a paper towel on the counter, he let her go reluctantly.

"Vain regrets," Elaine said, wiping her face and trying to smile. "I'm such a fool. What good does it do to cry?"

He ignored the question, putting an arm around her and leading her toward the living room. "I've made up the fire," he said gruffly. "Suppose you come in with me and tell me what this is all about."

Elaine went with him willingly, and when he pulled her down into his lap in the big chair, she made only a token resistance.

"This is silly," she said, half struggling. "I may be acting like a child, but I'm not one. Let me sit in another chair."

"I want you close," Bruce said, still

gruff. "Don't worry, I'm not making a move on you . . . not yet. Now, what was all that? You could have stopped who from doing what?"

Elaine sighed. Feeling drained, yet somehow better than she had in days, she leaned back in the crook of his arm and turned so she could see his face.

"I could have stopped Frank from killing himself," she said unevenly. "I could have, but I didn't. I . . . I put it off, and when I finally came here it was too late."

Bruce looked at her in total amazement. "What in God's name makes you think he killed himself? A man doesn't drape himself in barbed wire . . . "

"Frank would." She sat up straighter. "He *did*. He made it look like an accident, that's all. He'd be too proud to want people to know he'd given up. He wrote to me . . . " She went on, telling him everything, finally getting up and bringing the note for him to see, sitting back down in his lap as if that was where she belonged.

"This proves nothing," Bruce said, disbelief still in his eyes, anger in his heart because she was hurting. "Even if it did, even if he killed himself, you aren't responsible. To commit suicide is a hard decision to make. If he'd made it, you couldn't have changed his mind."

"He might have listened to me," Elaine said bleakly. "He might even have written the note just to see if I cared enough . . . and I didn't. Not even enough to t-try to keep him a-alive . . . "

Bruce pulled her against him and let the new tears seep into his shirt. He waited for a few minutes and then spoke carefully. "I still think it was an accident, Elaine. There's no proof in that note."

"The proof is in the facts," she said wearily, wiping her eyes. "He'd lost all his money. Frank could never have faced that alone. For the first time, he really needed someone."

Bruce was silent, thinking. It was possible, whether he liked it or not. The note could be interpreted that way. But guilt was torturing her — or was it only guilt? An unreasonable jealousy seared through him.

"Did you still love him?"

She sat up. "No." The wet eyes looked

57

away, he could see her struggling to find words, and then she burst out, "I suppose that's the real reason I feel so guilty. I *never* loved him. I was eighteen, in love with love; in love with the idea of a rich, handsome man wanting me. He was twenty-eight and I thought he was mature and wise, but he wasn't. I wanted out a month after we were married. Then I grew up, but Frank never did. He lived only for pleasure, and I don't think he ever had a serious thought." Her eyes came back and met Bruce's, pleading for understanding. "Do you know how *boring* that can be? That and his women." She stopped and took a breath, then added stubbornly, "Still, I shouldn't have let him die."

Bruce let out his breath softly. "You aren't making sense. What you're saying is that he wrote that note as a subtle cry for help, yet you've described him as a completely self-centered, hedonistic man who used the world as a playground. A man like that isn't subtle — he demands what he wants. To me, that note has an overtone of triumph. He'd found his way out. I think he had some plan that would let him go on living the way he wanted to live."

Elaine stared at him, considering this entirely different view, then shook her head. "That's impossible. He had no marketable skills, no ability at all to make money. He would have had to rob a bank. Maybe several banks." She sighed, rubbing her face with both hands in a childlike gesture. "Still, you may have been right in saying I couldn't have stopped him. Frank would have utterly hated being poor. He wouldn't have thought an ordinary life worth living." She slid from his lap and stood up, trying for calmness. "Would you like another cup of coffee?"

Bruce wanted to reach out, draw her back into his lap, and drive the last thought of Frank Jeffrey from her mind. But, looking at her, he couldn't risk trying. "Sounds good," he said casually, and watched her stride away, back straight, braid swinging, in control again. But she had trusted him enough to tell him; she had felt comforted in his arms. For a beginning, that was enough, and he was intensely grateful for it. Courting

Elaine Jeffrey was like hunting a shy, wild creature. A soft-eyed doe, alert to the first sign of pursuit, slipping away at the rustle of a leaf. Hurt once, he thought, and forever wary. But not as wary now. He had felt her slender body relax and grow warm in his arms.

* * *

"We need fresh air." Bruce put down his coffee cup, the fourth of the day. "We need exercise. And the wind has stopped. Go find some boots and a coat." He stood up, stretching, and grinned down at Elaine's drowsy look. She was curled up in the big chair, supple as a kitten, about to go to sleep. It was after lunch, a big, very late lunch that had included a large roast and vegetables, plus a mixed salad. Elaine had cooked all morning in a frenzy of action that was, he knew, designed to keep her occupied. She had withdrawn from their earlier intimacy, and while he understood it, he hadn't liked it. He'd paced restlessly through the house, wanting her in his arms again. He could still feel her softness, could still smell the alluring, feminine scent of her skin, and it had sharpened his desire to a positive ache.

Elaine yawned elaborately. She wasn't as sleepy as she was pretending to be. It just seemed safer. She had recognized Bruce's restlessness easily — she was having the same symptoms herself. His big body drew her like a magnet; she felt his every glance like a ray of sun, her skin warming where it touched. Only purely instinctive female resistance had kept her from dropping into his lap again when they'd come out here after lunch. Now, she sat up and smoothed her hair, smiling at him.

"A good idea. I'll see what warm clothes I can find." Fresh air and exercise. Wasn't that the recommended cure for frustration? She almost ran up the stairs.

There was a pullover wool sweater, a thick, heavily padded coat that came down past her hips, a pair of knee-high, patent-leather boots, a gold knitted cap, and what seemed to be a mile of matching gold scarf. She put them all on and clumped down the stairs, lost in the bundle. In a sharp reaction to the sad emotion of the morning, she felt full of giddy gaiety, her huge eyes sparkling like silver.

"If I topple over, you'll have to set me on my feet again."

Waiting in his hooded mackinaw, Bruce grinned. "Do you rock back and forth if you're pushed? I like toys."

She strutted past him in an imitation of a mechanical walk. "I-am-a-toy," she said, falsetto. "Play-with-me."

"I'd love to," he breathed, but she was out, streaking through the door and floundering along in a big drift of snow, giggling. Bruce followed, plowing after her, catching up as she flung herself down on her back and moved straightened arms up and down, drawing angel wings in the snow. Grinning, he waited until she had finished and then took her outstretched hands and pulled her straight up, leaving a perfect imprint of a snow angel.

"Too fat," he said critically.

"That's his heavenly robes, Elaine said indignantly. "Don't you know anything?" Reaching down, she cupped snow in her hands threateningly and watched him leap away, his long legs plunging and soaring over the deep snow. Then he crouched and started making a snowball of his own.

The battle raged while the storm drifted away, the wind now only a whisper, the last few white flakes falling lazily through air that vibrated with wild yells and laughter. Panting, Elaine finally called a truce.

"Enough! Let's go look at the valley."

Trudging around the house, they climbed the outside steps to the narrow balcony and looked out over the fairyland of glistening white far below to the pale peaks rising beyond. Bruce pointed to the yellow shape of a utility truck on the valley road beneath them.

"Someone must have lost their power," he commented, watching the moving dark dots of men. "They're laying line. Must have been miserable in this weather."

Elaine shivered. "Makes me cold just to think of it. Let's go in."

Retracing the path they made, they went back to the front and reentered a dark and rapidly chilling house. Startled, they looked at each other and broke into wry laughter.

"I'll call," Bruce said, "but we've probably been cut off until they repair that line. Go in by the fire and take off your damp coat."

Elaine looked at him thoughtfully. "I think there's a propane lantern in the storage room. I'll get it."

"No, it's too cold out there. I'll take care of everything, love. You stay by the fire." He looked down at her with what she could only describe as an indulgent expression. She liked the little, casual *love*, but the indulgence she could do without.

"Don't belittle me," she said crisply. "We'll work together. Since I know where the lantern is, I'll get it."

Bruce's eyebrows rose. She looked small and cold, peering out of that damp bundle of clothes in the darkened foyer, but he knew she wasn't weak; he remembered the surprising strength of her slim arms around his waist. He grinned suddenly and grabbed her under the bulky sleeves of the padded coat, lifted her into the air, and looked into her startled face.

"By golly, you're right! You're as big as I am. Mind if I kiss you? Of course you don't."

Elaine gasped, feeling his mouth take hers, feeling the soft beard against her skin, the flick of his tongue between her lips. Then he had set her down again, laughing.

"Go get the lantern, tiger, while I call the utility company. This place isn't getting any hotter."

She went, speechless and flushed, warmer than she had any right to be in damp clothes and a cool house. She shouldn't have let him . . . *let* him? He was as quick as he was strong; she hadn't had a chance to stop him. Lifting the lantern down from its shelf, she found a rag and wiped the dust from it, beginning to smile. Why stop him? It had been a very pleasant kiss — between friends.

Going in, she met Bruce coming out for firewood. "What did they say?"

The brown eyes still held a warm amusement. "They said three or four hours, five max. I say five. Now for the bad news. There was even more snow in town. They're working on it, but we're stuck here until they get to the mountain roads. Estimated time of arrival is four P.M. tomorrow."

Elaine made a sound of sympathetic dismay. "Then you'll have to miss another day at your office."

The brown eyes flickered. "Doesn't matter," he said cheerfully. "I called this morning and told them I'm taking extra time off." He touched her cheek lightly with the tips of his fingers. "Hey, cold! Get in by the fire."

A half hour later, they had created a circle of warmth around the fire. The propane lantern glowed in the background on a strategically placed table; piled against the side of the fireplace were enough logs to last the night. The double doors to the foyer had been closed, the kitchen shut off, the heavy draperies pulled across the wall of glass. The fire roared, radiating a heat that warmed the big room in spite of the high ceiling.

Elaine had made a mad dash to her icy bedroom and changed into dry jeans and

66

the thick, wildly colored socks, and now she sat cross-legged on the thick rug at the hearth and brushed out her damp braid of red-brown hair. It shimmered and glowed in the firelight as she twisted it up again, pressing in the big tortoiseshell pins absently.

Bruce had been to the liquor cabinet and had returned with a squat bottle of brandy. He handed her a glass and dropped down beside her with his own.

"What do you think of our cave?"

Elaine laughed. "It's the finest cave this side of prehistory. Good thing I made that roast today; we can have sandwiches later." She looked at him, watched the firelight flicker on his strong face, and thought how caring Bruce was, how sensitive to her feelings, and how much fun with that quick sense of humor. There was a lot more to him than just that compelling face and the big body that made her pulse quicken. Impulsively, she raised her glass to him.

"To you," she said softly, "because you stayed. Oh, I suppose I could have managed by myself, but I would have been scared and lonely. You've been great, Bruce. A real friend."

Maybe it was too soon, but he had to take the chance. They'd be out of here tomorrow evening. He turned to her, his mouth smiling, his eyes serious. "A friend? I want a lot more than that from you, Elaine. Is that all you want from me?"

In the split-second before she answered him, Elaine had time to wonder at how quickly her decision had come when she hadn't even known she was making one. She put her glass down and reach for him.

"No. This, too, please."

Bruce's glass rolled away, and brandy spilled in a golden stream as he took her offered mouth and pulled her into his arms. There was nothing casual about this kiss; his stored-up hunger for her took over in deep, satisfying possession. His lips welded to the soft, sensuous curves of hers, he searched and savored the yielding inner flesh until he felt her relax against him, felt her tongue curl over his invitingly, coaxing for more. Then, with a deep, incoherent sound, he drew away. His hands went to her knotted hair, tossed aside the heavy pins, and let the shining mass flood down over his fingers. Tilting her head, he looked into her eyes.

"Sure?" he asked unevenly. "Absolutely sure?"

Elaine smiled, the gray eyes dark with promise. "Positive," she whispered. "I want you very much."

He let out his breath, tension flowing from his tightened muscles. Settling her across his chest, he kissed her again, moving his warm mouth exploringly over her face, the soft beard a new erotic dimension she loved. Then, still quivering from his kisses, Elaine felt his hand grasp the bottom of her velour pullover and raise it. Propping her against his raised knees, he drew the pullover over her head in a smooth motion, baring her to the waist and exposing her breasts, taut and gleaming in the shadowy light.

"I've had fantasies about you," he murmured huskily, then eased her back against his chest again, cradling her in his arm. "This is one of them. You with me in front of the fire, your hair loose and streaming over my arm, your breasts bare in my hand . . . "

His deep voice was as seductive as his caresses, as his exploring fingers wandered over the curves of her aroused breasts, and his rough palm teased the sensitive nipples. Wave after wave of desire rippled through her, warmly enticing. She moved sinuously against the stroking palm, her own fingers slipping through the buttons of his shirt to move over hard, firm flesh and thread luxuriantly through the coarse mat of curls.

"I had a fantasy myself," she murmured, "concerning a half-naked man in a skimpy red silk robe. But I need your chest bare." She moved again, leaning against his knee, her eyes shining as she watched him remove his shirt. Then she leaned forward with a small sound of desire and clung to him, her now-aching breasts pressed into the tight curls, her open mouth teasing his, her tongue flickering between his firm lips.

"Oh, Lord . . . " Lying back on the rug, taking her with him, he clenched her slim body between his thighs. "Better than any dream," he said thickly, "unless this is a dream . . . " He grasped her

70

waist and lifted her, feeling her fragrant hair sweep his face, raising her farther until her breasts touched his mouth. Then he rolled, easing her to the rug beside him, smoothing her hair away from her face, kissing the panting mouth tenderly before moving to her white breasts.

"Snow angel . . . " His bearded face pressed against the creamy mound, and his hot mouth closed over the taut tip.

Elaine gasped for breath, looking down at the dark head silhouetted by the fire, feeling the exquisite jolts of sensation as he suckled. Shakily, she lifted her hands and fastened her fingers in his rough hair, holding him close.

"Bruce . . . Bruce . . . " She hardly recognized the soft, ragged sound as her own voice, urgent and wanting. When he moved to kiss her mouth again and his massive chest slid against her wet and glistening breasts, she could feel the wild thunder of his heartbeat blending with hers. Then he was rising between her and the fire like a huge genie, sitting back and straddling her legs, his hands at the waistline of her jeans.

A tremor of doubt shuddered through her and was burned away in the flames of desire. There was that certain knowledge that once she gave herself to him nothing would be the same again, but at this moment there was nothing she wanted more than his possession. She lifted her hips, helping him to slide the rest of her clothes down and away. The jeans, the scrap of bikini panties, and the wild socks all fell from his hand into a heap on the floor, and he was sitting back, looking at her, touching her with light, shaping strokes.

"Elaine." Bruce was having trouble with his voice. Seeing that exquisite small body had shaken him. He knew her so well now in other ways. Her tears, her laughter, her sorrows and courage. But this . . . his eyes went to hers. "You are giving me so much beauty . . . "

There was no room for doubt. "Then give me you," she said softly, and held out her arms.

"You already have me." He bent, running kisses from her satiny belly to her waiting lips, then pulled away to take off his own clothes. Settling down beside her, pulling her against his aroused body, he added huskily, "You've had me since you opened the door of this house." He smiled, no longer uncertain. "Now, what are you going to do with me?"

It was a wonder. Now that they lay naked together there was no more tension, no real urgency. She smiled back at him, touching his bearded cheek lightly.

"That's easy. I'm going to make love with you, as much love as possible." She felt the involuntary movement of his loins against her and smiled again. "Starting right now, I think."

He took her so carefully. In the end, it was her own arching eagerness that joined them completely, her utter abandon that drew him past the edge of control. Then, a little awed by this strength, she felt the full force of his passion sweep over her, felt the subtle skill of his tireless body take her thrust by thrust into a shattering, delicious fulfillment that echoed and echoed again, throbbing away so slowly she thought it might never end.

Murmuring, touching, they lay together

until the increasing chill of the air made Bruce lift his head and look at the fire, now no more than smoldering coals. He rose, taking logs to build it up again, while Elaine, deprived of the heat of his body, shivered her way back into her clothes. She thought he looked magnificent in the flickering light of the lantern and growing fire: he was naked power moving back and forth unconcernedly. Another fantasy — the cave, and the man who protected it. She watched curiously as he took tongs and scraped a pile of hard, glowing coals to one side.

"What are you doing?"

He turned and grinned. "That's for the coffee pan. Ever drink boiled coffee? It's good if you make it right."

The thought made her suddenly, immensely hungry. "And sandwiches! We can make them out here." She turned toward the kitchen and whirled back, coming to put her arms around his neck and kiss him. "You're beautiful," she said softly. "You're the best thing that ever happened to me." Then she was gone, uttering a small yelp of dismay as she entered the icy kitchen.

Bruce reached for his jeans, knowing he'd never been happier. She was all he'd ever wanted, but he was afraid to push his luck. She was caught up in the thrilling happiness of fulfilled lovemaking right now, but he sensed that trouble lay ahead for her. There would be too much on her mind to press her about the future. He would have to be patient . . . ever so patient.

4

A PALE yellow sun hung in a patch of ice-blue sky over snow-covered peaks and set a shaft of light through a crack between the draperies in the master bedroom. Elaine's long black lashes fluttered from the intrusion but refused to open. She was entirely too comfortable otherwise, her body cradled neatly by a warm, breathing wall behind her. She was thinking, or maybe just drowsily remembering.

It had been almost midnight when the lights sprang on in the big room downstairs and the comforting hum of the heating system had informed them that the ordeal by cold was over. In a half hour, the house was warm enough to go to bed, and Bruce had banked the fire, put up the screen, and hauled her out of her chair by one hand.

At the top of the stairs, Elaine had automatically turned toward the room she'd been using, and Bruce had laughed at her, still firmly holding on to her hand.

"Are you kidding?" he had asked, and tugged her toward the other end of the hall. Half asleep, Elaine had given him a foolish grin.

"Watch the arm," she'd said. "Remember who stirs the pot."

Still laughing, Bruce had let go of her hand and reached behind her, grabbing a thick handful of silky hair, leaving his arm across her back, urging her forward. She'd sighed happily and leaned into his side, putting her arm around his waist, going with him willingly, oh, so willingly, to the bed where he slept. Their lovemaking had been every bit as satisfactory as the first time. No, even better. She let her thoughts dwell on the little, intimate things that had made it better, and she felt a tendril of warmth growing upward from her loins like a tropical vine.

Carefully, since from the deep, even breathing against her back she was sure Bruce was still sleeping, she eased away and lay flat, turning her head cautiously to look at him through a tangle of red-brown hair. Her heart contracted, as if someone had given it a gentle squeeze. Even with the beard, he had a look of youth and vulnerability, qualities she'd never before seen in his face. The deep brown eyes that seemed to know so much were closed, the strong features softened by sleep, the black hair spilling untidily over his forehead. She had a crazy but earnest desire to put her arms around him, draw him over to her shoulder, and hold him there like a sleepy child. Then, looking at the massive shoulders and chest only half hidden by the covers, her mouth curved in amusement at her thoughts. She'd need a derrick. Or maybe she could simply slide over and nudge her shoulder under him.

She sighed softly. It would only wake him up. She went on looking at him, letting her eyes travel down the miniature mountain range he made under the amber blanket, let them travel back up slowly to his face, where they met an open brown gaze as warm as her thoughts. She smiled, and a large hand snaked under the covers and grasped her waist, pulling her close.

The bearded face fell quite naturally into the curve of her shoulder, proving that any problem could be solved by a little cooperation. Satisfied, she put her arms around his neck and held him.

"That was a lovely smile." His voice was blurred but contented.

"I was having lovely thoughts."

"Mmm." His mouth opened and then closed on her shoulder, munching sensuously along a line to her neck, where it fastened like that of a fangless Dracula. She felt his muscular leg move over her, bend, and clasp her thighs neatly against his loins. He had been having lovely thoughts, too.

She snuggled closer, and the phone rang.

They drew back and looked at each other, and then she was scrambling from bed, looking wildly for something to put on, grabbing up his shirt and running out, leaving the door open.

Bruce listened shamelessly.

"Hello? Oh — yes, I know I haven't called. I thought it was going to last another day . . . Tonight? Well, I suppose I could — it would be a good idea to get started, since I have to leave soon . . . ”

Bruce frowned. Fenton, setting up the first meeting. With *his* woman, who was still so mixed up, so raw with her crazy guilt. He sighed and got up out of bed, heading for the shower.

Elaine was just turning away from the phone when he came down the hall, still damp, wearing a towel wrapped around his narrow hips and carrying his jeans. She looked pale again, her lips drawn straight, her eyes haunted.

“Is Al Fenton always so mysterious?” she asked, her brows drawing together. “He’s talked all this time without telling me anything except that I should be prepared for some surprises. He’s had the will and a lot of other things sent here from his office . . . ” She stopped, her eyes focusing on Bruce, her face clearing, beginning to smile. “Aren’t you cold?”

“I’m on my way to the laundromat,” Bruce said with dignity. “I’ll trouble you for that shirt you’re wearing.”

“Oh.” She looked down at the heavy black-and-red-plaid folds that hung to her knees. She hadn’t bothered to button

80

it, since first she would have had to find her hands in the sleeves. She slipped it off and handed it to him, watching his startled eyes take in every bare inch. She knew he'd thought she'd run to her room for something else before she gave it up, and it pleased her to reach up and smooth back her hair, turn around slowly, and stroll toward her room. "Start the coffee," she said sweetly, putting a little subtle movement in her rounded buttocks. "I'll be down in a minute." She was at the door before he moved.

"You look better without it," he said hoarsely, and turned blindly toward the stairs.

Showered and dressed, Elaine brought the skimpy robe with her when she came down. Pouring coffee with one hand, Bruce was using the other to hold his rapidly slipping towel. She helped him into the robe and picked up the towel.

"I like you in red silk," she said thoughtfully. "With all that black beard and curly chest hair, you look like an oversized maharaja. Sexy." She grinned at him. Jeaned and braided, fresh and clear-eyed, she had lost the haunted look.

81

Bruce bent and kissed her.

"I'm going with you this evening."

Elaine looked startled and then frowned. Taking her cup to the table, she sat down and looked at Bruce. "It's a dinner meeting. In fact, Al said they wanted me to spend the night, maybe two nights, until we finish sorting things out."

Sitting down opposite her, Bruce ran his hand distractedly through his hair. "And did you agree to that?"

She smiled suddenly. "No. I didn't even promise I'd be there tonight. I only said if the roads were cleared I'd try. I thought you might not be leaving until tomorrow."

Bruce looked up, seeing the open warmth in those wide, soft silver eyes. Her meaning was plain; if he was going to be here, she wanted to be with him. None of the usual coquettish sparring, none of the games most women played at the beginning of an affair. Just an honest declaration of desire. A wave of heat ran over him, and he shifted restlessly in the chair, willing himself to be patient.

"I'm not leaving," he said abruptly, "so we'll go together. I want to hear these surprises Fenton has for you. Did he give you any hints?"

"No, except to say it wasn't all bad news." She was looking at him curiously. "Bruce, I'm sure I can handle it alone. I appreciate your concern, but why mix yourself up in such a dismal business? It shouldn't take long — I think Fenton is just trying to make it sound important."

"Maybe," Bruce said slowly, "but I don't like it. If there's a will, it should be cut and dried — no problems. But he seems to be making some, and if you don't mind, I'll invite myself to the Fenton dinner."

Looking at him, Elaine wondered if she'd mind anything he did. Leave, maybe. At least he wasn't in a rush to do that. "I think I'll like it," she said, smiling. "What a ploy, bringing a lawyer of my own." She stood up, turning to the refrigerator. "What would you like with your next cup of coffee? Ham and eggs, or fruit and Danish?"

"Ham and eggs," he said promptly. "I plan to be active."

After pushing up the sleeves of a cream-colored knit, another of her favorite boat-neck and oversized cotton shirts, Elaine set about frying thick slices of ham to a turn, bringing out eggs to scramble, and heating up small, flaky croissants to have with them. She was half smiling, confident. This morning when she'd stepped from the shower, she had taken the time to really look at her body. Reasonably pleased by what she saw, she had dressed, she hoped, appropriately. These were designer jeans, cut to make her curves more enticing. The knit top was soft and figure-molding, and there was nothing under it except a quick spray of Anaïs Anaïs, a sexy perfume someone had given her at the last office party. She had hesitated about braiding her hair, wondering if she should leave it loose, then decided not to be blatant. Again, that was. She'd already been blatant when she gave Bruce his shirt.

Watching her, Bruce began to realize that he had taken part in a reawakening. Some long-held barrier had gone crashing down. She was so different. It was as if part of that lovely and warm something inside had emerged, flaunting itself proudly. Every move she made, from the way she walked to the way she glanced at him, was openly provocative, warmly sensual. When she leaned over him to place his filled plate in front of him, her breast brushed his shoulder, her own fresh scent mingled with some earthy perfume she wore. It was all he could do to keep from dragging her down into his lap and skipping breakfast entirely. She was a living, breathing temptation, and she was doing it deliberately. He loved it, and loved it more when she sat down opposite him and he saw that the brief contact had affected her, too. Beneath the soft, cream-colored knit, tiny points pressed out at him invitingly. Fortunately, his loins were hidden by the table. Draped in thin red silk, his own reaction was spectacular.

He forced himself to begin to eat. He did love it; he could hardly wait to get her back into bed. But it wasn't enough. He talked, praising the food and making a few remarks about the weather, and went right on thinking about the way he felt. It was new, something different for him. From this woman he wanted everything. Desire, yes, and trust — he knew he was doing well in those departments. But she could feel those things and still walk away again, into her own life. He needed her love. It was frightening to think that by her own admission she had never loved, and he had to have that. For the first time in his life, he was in love, and he damned well wanted the feeling returned.

Calmer, he finished the last of his coffee and stood up. "Great breakfast," he said. "Thank you. I guess I'll put my clothes in the dryer." He went past her to the cubicle at the end of the kitchen and transfered the jeans and heavy shirt to the dryer, came back, and stopped as he saw her busily loading the dishwasher. "Need some help?"

She turned and smiled. How could he look ridiculous and magnificent at the same time in that red silk? "No, this won't take a minute." Her jaw dropped a little as he nodded unconcernedly and strolled out, heading for the stairs. Hastily finishing her task, she wiped slim hands on a dish towel and hurried after him.

Standing at the window in his bedroom,

Bruce stared unseeingly at the glittering white world outside and listened for her footsteps. His tense shoulders dropped in relief as he heard her open the door and come in.

"I . . . I thought I'd make your bed," she said breathlessly.

He turned toward her, seeing the shy but eager stance of her slender body, hesitating in the middle of the room, seeing the wide, silvery eyes fixed on him hopefully, the full, parted lips, the quick rise and fall of her breasts as she waited for him to speak or move. His arms opened.

"Make my day, instead."

She went into his arms with a deep sigh, hugging him, her hands slipping down to the hard buttocks, more erotic than ever in their silken covering. His response was instantaneous, thrusting hard against her belly, and he felt the quick, answering tilt of her hips, a sinuous brushing against him. *Make my day? God, Make my life* . . . He picked her up and took her to the bed, putting her down and closing his lips over hers fiercely, filling her mouth with his tongue, deep, slow thrusts that brought her arms up tight around him, asking for more. When he drew away, her eyes were slumberous with desire, her face flushed and happy. He was half sitting on the bed, leaning over her, and she drew her fingertips down over his chest, untied the robe, and pushed it aside.

"Mmm." She touched him, her small hand tentative at first, only her fingertips sliding over his aroused loins, threading through the tight curls at the bottom of his abdomen. Then her smooth palm shaped itself around the hot erection with sensuous caresses.

Shuddering with desire, Bruce pushed both big hands up under her loose shirt to grasp and knead her breasts while he bent and kissed her again, sucking her lips, one by one, into his mouth to roll and nip ravenously.

"What do you like best?" Elaine was whispering, straining upward against the weight of his chest. She put both hands in his hair and moaned with pleasure as he pushed the shirt up and took her breasts in his mouth with the same ravenous intensity. "Oh-h-h . . . oh, I want to please *you*, Bruce. Tell me how."

He raised his head and looked at her, then sat up and pulled her into his arms, holding her tightly. "I want you to love me," he said huskily, "that's all. Just love me, Elaine."

"Oh, I will." She drew away, her eyes dark and shining, and stood up, pulling her shirt off over her head, unzipping the jeans and stepping out of them. Tugging the straining robe from his shoulders, she drew him down with her on the bed, holding him, her face pressed against his neck. Her voice was muffled. "You've done so much for me, Bruce. I feel like a woman again . . . as if I've come back to life." Her hand trailed over him caressingly. "You're absolutely wonderful." She raised herself suddenly on her elbows and hovered over him, her hair falling on his neck. Her eyes were enormous dark pools, her mouth smiling, the lips parted enough to show the glistening small teeth, the tip of her tongue. There was a kittenish growl in her voice as she went on, "I know. I'll love you all over and find out for myself what you like best."

He turned to her, bending around her,

his hands stroking her satiny back as she began to caress him. It wasn't what he had meant, but he wasn't about to turn it down.

★ ★ ★

In the middle of the afternoon, Elaine made a long-distance call, talking for some time to her employer in South Carolina. Then she came back into the big room and found Bruce standing at the wall of glass, staring down thoughtfully at the valley. She joined him, looking out, too.

"I've lost my job."

He looked down at her disconsolate face and was tempted to say it now. A dozen phrases ran through his mind, confused and jumbled. *You won't need one when we're married . . . forget it, I want you with me . . . I'll take care of you.* But it was too soon, and he knew it. She hadn't even begun to consider a future with him. He took refuge in anger.

"The bastard."

Elaine shook her head. "Not really. It's

a very small operation, and the budget's tight. He's waited, hiring part-time help by the hour, and it's just too expensive. I can't blame him." She lifted her chin and smiled. "I'll find another job, Bruce. He said he'd give me excellent references. You don't have to worry about me." There was a great deal of confidence in her voice that wasn't reflected in her eyes. She had started out late in the job market after those years of marriage, and this had been her first decent position. She was scared, he knew, and trying her best to hide it. He shoved his hands in his pockets to keep from taking her in his arms.

"There's a demand in Atlanta for good secretaries," he said cautiously. "I might be able to help you find a place there."

She laughed and slipped her hand through his arm, hugging him to her. "You really are kind, Bruce. But you don't have to take me on as a charity case. You've done more than enough for me now."

Her touch was too much for him. His hand came out of his pocket and went around her, holding her close. "What about what you've done for me? You've given me so much, darling. So much beauty, so much pleasure." He couldn't say *love*, not yet.

Her face stilled, growing serious. "No strings attached, Bruce. We've enjoyed each other, that's all." Then, in a quick change of mood, she laughed suddenly and leaned against him. "And we'll probably keep it up very enthusiastically until one of us leaves. The storm made us a little world of our own, didn't it?"

Bruce suddenly saw it from her point of view. They had actually known each other only three days, and that was her reference point. The storm had isolated them as if they were in a time capsule, and they'd gained an intimacy that would normally have taken months, but while she realized that, she still saw them as virtual strangers. But he didn't. He felt as if he'd known her forever, had loved her all his life. But, then, he'd felt that way since the moment she'd opened the door. He couldn't blame that on the storm. His arm tightened. "Yes," he said gruffly, "we have had our own world. And I keep wishing that snow blower down there would turn around and go back to town. I'm not sure I want to rejoin the rest of the human race just yet."

Elaine followed Bruce's gaze, seeing the cleared roads in the valley like black ribbons in the snow, and the white plume rising as the heavy machine inched closer and closer to the beginning of the road that led upward. Her smile disappeared; her eyes clouded as she moved away from him, looking at the clock on the mantel.

"It looks as if we'll make it," she said. "The Fentons expect me at eight, and the roads will be clear hours before then." She looked back at him. "Maybe I'm feeling the same way you are. I know I ought to be glad I can get on with what I have to do, but I'm not glad at all. I feel as if I'm leaving a safe and happy place. I think you've spoiled me."

He left the wall of glass and came to put an arm around her, leading her to the chairs by the fire. Sitting, he pulled her into his lap. "Practice session," he said, "in feeling safe and happy, so we'll know how wherever we are."

She yielded to his embrace with a low sound of contentment, her mouth opening under his without urging. Bruce kissed her possessively, knowing he was grasping at straws to read more meaning into her words than she said, but it wouldn't hurt to spoil her a little more.

5

AT five-thirty, Bruce finished shoveling the drifts of snow away from the garage door, raised it, and brought out the big, powerful wagon. The heavy snow tires churned through the thickly covered parking area and down the driveway, where he stopped long enough to shovel the drifts from the log entrance. Coming back up, he reported to Elaine that the road below was clear.

"There will be patches of ice this evening," he added, "but we'll have the wagon. I'd like to leave in an hour and drop you off at Fenton's so I can change at the club. I'm getting a bit tired of this shirt and these jeans."

In spite of his smile, Elaine thought he seemed different, as if he had his mind on the coming evening. She thought of arriving with him at Al Fenton's home, early and unannounced, and felt a bit tense herself.

"Won't it seem strange to them when

we arrive together?" she asked. "What possible excuse can we give them?"

He grinned. "I'm buying the house, and I came by to see how you made out. My car is clearly better for driving in this weather. Any other excuse we need I'll think up when we need it."

Elaine thought he probably could. Lawyers had to learn to think on their feet. Anyway, it didn't matter what the Fentons thought if they were polite enough to keep it to themselves. Running upstairs to dress, she wondered why she had taken such a dislike to Al Fenton. Because he talked too much and said nothing? Or because the way he bent over her made her feel trapped? Childish reasons. Showering, she decided to reserve judgment.

She wavered over what to wear. A dinner, but hardly a festive occasion. She still had a few good things; she chose a suit from among them, a silver-gray velveteen with a straight skirt and a swinging, fur-lined cape with a hood. With her hair up, the high-necked white silk blouse, and a pair of suede pumps, she had only to take off the frivolous cape to look extremely discreet.

"You look beautiful," Bruce told her, handing her into the wagon, "but untouchable. That's the exact color of chain mail."

She gave him a very small smile and waited until he got in to answer. "Why do I wish I *did* have a suit of armor? Al Fenton has been very courteous to me, but I still feel he's hiding his real feelings. I suppose that he and his wife are both very critical of me."

Driving out, Bruce looked at Elaine in surprise. "Why? I understood they were strangers to you."

"They are. I'd never seen Fenton until we met at the inquest, and I still haven't met his wife, but Frank often spoke of them. I didn't mix much with his friends, but I did get the impression that they were very close. Usually close friends blame a broken marriage on the other partner."

Bruce shrugged, turning down the steep driveway, following the deep ruts he'd made earlier. "People take that sort of thing lightly these days." He glanced over at her, knowing she didn't. It was

97

probably part of her overall sense of guilt, and this meeting with Jeffrey's friends had brought it back. He was suddenly very glad he'd insisted on going along. He'd seen Fenton in court, and the man could be overbearing, almost vicious when he sensed a weak point.

The Fenton home was just outside the little town, in a section of rather pretentious 'vacation cottages.' The Fentons, Bruce knew, were like half the population — here only parts of the year, either for the cool summer months or the hunting season. As a rule, wives and children spent most of the summer; the men came for hunting in fall and winter. Evidently, Beth Fenton had stayed on this year.

The house was situated on a gentle rise. The driveway had been cleared of snow and was easy to find. Bruce wheeled up to the front door at seven, looked over at Elaine's tense and unhappy face, reached over, and clasped her hand.

"Stop worrying, angel. The Fentons are civilized, and, anyway, I'll be back as soon as I change."

"I wouldn't call it worrying," Elaine

said bleakly. "I just don't like this." She glanced at him as he opened his door. "Bruce . . . they may not ask you to come back." She wished he would stay, rough clothes and all.

He grinned suddenly, stepping out. "They will. Al will insist. You'll see." He went around and opened her door. "Come along. I just saw a drapery move. They're spying on us."

Elaine laughed, getting out and taking his arm. He made it sound like a mystery movie instead of just the dreary business of settling the muddled affairs of a dead man. She was still smiling as Al Fenton opened the door, blinking at them in amazement. His tall, lanky body was clad in a casual shirt and a pair of old wool trousers, his thin blond hair disarranged in the back as if he'd been snoozing in a lounge chair.

"Well, this is a surprise. Hello, you two. Come in." He had managed, Elaine noted, to find his pleasant smile.

The front door opened directly into a large room that evidently served as both living and dining room and ran the length of the house. It was furnished in a typically rustic style, with hand-hewn wooden furniture, upholstered in homespun. Mountain crafts of wood, bits of weaving, and pottery were scattered around the room on tables and hanging on the walls. Elaine's swift glance made a circuit of the room and back to Al Fenton's face as he took her coat. He was looking at Bruce.

"This is really odd," Al said, laughing a little. "I didn't even know you and Mrs. Jeffrey were acquainted, McClure."

Bruce grinned cheerfully. "Well acquainted, Al. I'm buying her house. And, by the way, Elaine has retained me to look out for her interests in settling her late husband's estate. I'm afraid I'll have to ask that you allow me to be present during any talk pertaining to that subject."

Speechless, Elaine stared at Bruce, then at Al. Al's narrow head had jerked up, his thin nostrils flared, his light blue eyes stony. Then he had turned, hanging Elaine's coat on a wall rack near the door, smiling as he turned back.

"Nothing simpler, Bruce. Stay to dinner. Beth and I both will be very glad to have you." He gestured toward a wide couch. "Have a seat, both of you, and I'll mix some drinks."

"Thanks, but I'm off to the club to change." Bruce still looked cheerful, very cheerful. "You're sure about the dinner, now? I'm not putting you out?"

Al shot him a sudden glance of pure, unguarded dislike. "Not a bit. In fact, I insist on you coming. See you later, then."

Still in a state of shock at having retained a lawyer without knowing it, Elaine moved to a chair as Al let Bruce out and shut the door. She sat down, swallowing a hysterical giggle. Then Al's thin figure was bending over her, his smile hospitable, his pale blue eyes blank.

"A martini, Elaine? Or do you prefer a highball?"

"Actually, I drink very little. I think I'll pass." She smiled up at him, wishing he'd move. "I should have called to say I was coming early, but Bruce was leaving and there really wasn't time. His car is so much better on icy roads." What a liar she was; and, for that matter, so was Bruce. But how do you say truthful things? *I don't like you, Al, and Bruce doesn't trust you, so we just did as we pleased.* No, it was better to lie.

"I understand perfectly," Al was saying, "and we're delighted to have you both. Could I pour you a glass of Perrier?"

Elaine assented, thinking Al wasn't doing too badly in the lie department either. He looked angry behind the smile, a bit shaken. Because of Bruce and that remark about 'looking out for her interests'? She had no interest in Frank's estate, except in seeing it properly executed. She watched Al go to a wet bar at the rear of the big room, mix himself a very dry martini, and pour a glass of Perrier over ice. He came back to her quickly, passing a half-open door near the wet bar that Elaine supposed led to the kitchen. Her quick ears had caught the sound of someone moving around inside there.

"I'm looking forward to meeting your wife," she said diplomatically as Al handed her the glass. "I hope the extra guest won't upset her plans."

Fenton sat down in the nearest chair and sipped his martini thirstily. "That won't upset Beth at all. But I should probably tell the cook." He rose again and, carrying his drink, went back to the half-open door and disappeared. In a moment, he came out again with that same quick stride and took a chair close to Elaine, settling into it nervously.

"Now I have a question," he said, his smile fixed on his face. "Tell me why you thought it necessary to retain McClure. Is something bothering you about Frank's estate?"

Play dumb. Elaine was reasonably sure Al shouldn't have asked that question, but since he had, she had to answer in some way. She raised her delicate brows and stared at him. "Isn't it the thing to do? Believe me, I have no idea of how to be an executrix, and I felt I needed legal advice. I hope I haven't offended you."

"Oh, not at all." He regarded her moodily and drained his glass. "However, I could have given you all the advice you need and saved you the extra expense. It's more a matter of bookkeeping this time, anyway. As you've probably found out, Frank had a lot of debts and — "

"I'm sorry," Elaine broke in hastily,

"but shouldn't we wait until Bruce is here to discuss this?"

Al colored. "I'm sure *he* would prefer it," he said sarcastically. "He'd like to appear to be earning his fee." He set his glass down and leaned forward. "Elaine, take it from me, you're wasting your money. You don't need a lawyer — *I'm* one! Dismiss him, and we'll have it settled in a matter of hours. He'll drag it out, hoping to earn more."

Play very *dumb*. "Oh, I doubt that," Elaine said carelessly, "Bruce is a very busy man. But I'll consider it, of course." She sipped her Perrier and looked around the room. "Your wife seems to find the mountain crafts very interesting. Isn't that a dulcimer?"

Al sat back, defeated. "I think so. The house was decorated when we bought it. Beth doesn't care much for it."

"I don't care much for what?" A door had opened behind them, and Beth Fenton had entered the room, tall, slim and very blond. She was wearing a dress of thin white wool, deeply cowled to display a thin gold necklace set with emeralds. Her shoulder-length pale blond hair was swept back to display more emeralds in her ears. She came forward, the softly cut dress swinging against a well-shaped bosom and long legs, to look down curiously at Elaine.

"The house," Al explained patiently, and stood up. "This is Elaine Jeffrey, Beth."

"Oh." Beth Fenton was clearly surprised. Greenish eyes narrowed and swung involuntarily to the clock and then came back to Elaine's face. "Well," she said gaily, dropping into the chair Al had vacated, "I suppose you must be, since Al tells me so, but you're certainly younger than I expected. How flattering that you came early to meet us. Has Al been entertaining you properly?" Without waiting for an answer, she looked up at Al with a bright smile. "If you'll fix drinks for us both, dear, you can safely leave Mrs. Jeffrey with me. You do need to dress, you know."

Without a word, Al picked up Elaine's nearly empty glass and went to the bar. In a few moments, he was back, handing his wife a martini and putting down a full glass of Perrier beside Elaine.

"We're having an extra guest, Beth," he said carefully. "Bruce McClure brought Elaine down the mountain and I invited him back for dinner."

Beth leaned back, tipping up her head to look at Al. "And you were planning to discuss business with Elaine after dinner. Well, that should put a stop to it."

"Hardly," Al said abruptly, turning away. "He's representing Elaine." He went on, heading for the door behind them.

Elaine had never been more uncomfortable in her life. She was on the verge of breaking into an apology for disrupting their plans when it occurred to her that the reason she was here was purely business. The Fentons might make a show of having a friendly dinner, but the undercurrents were telling a different story. She was suddenly glad Bruce had said what he had, lie or not. She looked up and met Beth's coldly startled look with a smile.

"It was so nice of Al to invite Bruce."

"And puzzling that you think you need him," Beth said frostily. "Don't you trust Al's judgment?" She sat forward suddenly. "Or was it Frank you didn't trust?" her voice rose angrily. "Do you honestly think Frank would treat you unfairly? Frank was never *mean* . . . in my opinion, he was too generous! My God, you'd *left* him . . . " She stopped, trying to control herself.

Somehow, Beth's hysterical, disconnected outburst calmed Elaine. She reminded herself that these two people had been among Frank's closest friends for years. Their emotions were probably more involved than hers. She looked away from the suddenly crumpled face, feeling more pity than anything else.

"You misunderstood," Elaine said quietly. "I want nothing at all from Frank's estate. But I don't know the first thing about settling it, and it looks like that's my job. I meant no insult to your husband, Beth. But I see nothing wrong in having another, impartial legal opinion."

Beth was still struggling with her feelings. "I should have kept my mouth shut," she mumbled, wiping her eyes carefully. "But it was all so tragic, and now it's just another cold piece of legal maneuvering." She reached for her glass and drained it, standing up. "That was stupid of me," she said dully. "Naturally, you're entitled to all the lawyers you want. Seems a funny choice, though, picking an outsider. Frank always used Harrison and Toth." She headed for the bar purposefully.

At the moment, Elaine was very glad her lawyer was an outsider, since she felt like one, too. She sat there staring into her glass and wondering if a person could refuse to execute a will. Or would that be cowardly? For the millionth time, she wished Frank had agreed to a divorce instead of a separation. She looked up as Beth returned with a brimming glass.

"This is a very pleasant house, Beth." She could at least try to change the subject. "So evocative of the mountains. Did you have any trouble during the storm?"

"Only with cabin fever," Beth said harshly. "Being cooped up in here nearly drove me up the wall. Al, of course, sat around and read." She sipped her new martini gloomily. "And slept. He sits and reads and then drops off to sleep. Not what you'd call exciting company." She sighed, leaning back. "How did you happen to meet Bruce McClure?"

Elaine was ready for that question; she had known one of them would ask. "Through Paul Somers," she said. "They've known each other for years." Paul had told her that — he and Bruce had grown up together. Now if Beth let it drop . . . She saw with relief the slight, indifferent shrug as Beth answered.

"I don't know anyone named Somers." Her tone indicated that someone she didn't know wasn't worth knowing. "I thought you might have known Bruce in Atlanta. He has a pretty impressive reputation there. Actually, I'm surprised he agreed to sit in on something as small as this." Her eyes ran over Elaine's face and slim figure speculatively. "It's probably just because he likes you."

Elaine smiled. This maliciousness she understood. "I hope so," she said calmly. "I like him."

The greenish eyes sharpened. "How long . . . " The sound of the doorbell cut her off, and she drained her glass again and stood up. "That's probably Bruce now."

Elaine relaxed as Beth went to the door. That next question was going to be sticky: How long have you known him? And the one after that might well have been: How *well* do you know him? — uttered with a smirk. She had a feeling that Beth's kitten claws could rapidly turn tigerish. And something was definitely bothering the tall blonde. Listening, Elaine could hear the coolness in Beth's voice at the door.

"How nice to see you again, Bruce. It's been ages."

Beth was taking a lined car coat from Bruce, hanging it up. Past her was Bruce's dark head, and Elaine felt that familiar gentle squeeze on her heart as she saw his smile flash in his dark beard. Then Beth was leading him into the room, and Elaine wondered if she really knew this man. In an understated, dark, English-cut suit, his hair and beard trimmed sleekly, Bruce was no longer a mountaineer. Maybe a diplomat.

"Sit down," Beth was saying, "I'll fix you a drink." She picked up her own glass and headed again for the bar, giving them a moment of privacy.

Elaine felt Bruce's hand cup the top of her head lightly as he passed and took the chair Beth had been using. "Everything all right?"

Elaine nodded and laughed softly. "You may not be comfortable in a three-piece suit," she said, sotto voce, "but it looks terrific on you."

He grinned at her. "Better than red silk?"

She choked a little on her Perrier. "No. But under the circumstances . . . "

They were laughing as Beth came back, handed a drink to Bruce, and sat down on a couch with her own refill. She was watching them, her eyes narrowed slightly, but as she started to speak the door behind them opened and Al came in. Smiling and urbane, he was wearing a mulberry jacket over dark slacks and a white shirt. Beth got to her feet again and started for the bar.

"Sit," she said to Al, gesturing to the couch. "I'll bring you a drink."

"I'll do it," Al said quickly, and he

reached out to stop her. "Let me, darling."

Beth shook his hand off, spilling her own drink. "I said *I* would," she answered, and went on, her heels tapping irritatedly.

Al sighed and sat down. "Well," he said to Bruce, "that was some storm, wasn't it?"

Caught again by the undercurrents between the Fentons, Elaine watched Beth's jerky, nervous movements across the room. Beth was gulping down an extra drink as she mixed another shaker, trying to keep it concealed. The men were still discussing the weather, but Elaine noticed Al's frequent glances toward the bar. Elaine sighed. Al undoubtedly was worried; he probably cared a great deal for his wife. Beth was definitely pretty, just short of beautiful because of the discontented lines around her mouth and the sharpness of her green eyes. And she was also definitely drinking too much. Finally, she turned, carrying a highball for Al and a full glass for herself, very careful now not to spill them. She stopped at the half-open door that apparently led to the kitchen and stood there for a moment, talking to someone. Then, joining the group again, she handed Al his drink and sipped hers before she sat down.

"Anyone who wants another drink before dinner," she said, "had better drink up. We'll be sitting down in ten minutes." Beth's eyes were very bright, her mouth smiling loosely. She tossed her hair back and looked at Elaine. "You really should have one of these martinis, Elaine. They're very good."

Elaine smiled and shook her head slightly, feigning an interest in the statistics about the storm that Al was reciting. In the background, a woman in black had come out and was efficiently setting a table, lighting candles. So, even in this little vacation house, Beth expected total service. But, then, Bruce had said she was used to great wealth. Elaine glanced at Beth, at the carefully madeup face and the bright eyes that were beginning to glaze. Beth was already hovering on the edge of real drunkenness, and suddenly Elaine hoped that the dinner would soon be served and consumed and the session afterward would be quick and easy. It was no time for another emotional breakdown.

The dinner was excellent, beginning with poached rainbow trout in a delicate sauce, followed by the entrée, a French casserole of chicken, herbs, and mushrooms. The imported white wine was dry but pleasantly fruity, and there was a green salad with a sharp, pungent dressing, accompanied by tiny hot rolls. Dessert was a light, chocolate soufflé served with espresso. Elaine enjoyed it all, but she couldn't keep her eyes off Beth Fenton. Beth made her way through the varied courses looking bored and eating very little, drinking the wine like water and holding out her glass for refills. She smiled vaguely as Bruce and Elaine both complimented her on the food.

"I take Emmeline wherever I go," she said, waving a careless hand at the silent woman in black. Her speech was slurred, her laugh unpleasant. "Not that Al cares — he'll eat anything. He has no palate, have you, dear?"

"Well," Al said defensively, pushing aside his plate, "I like a good steak. Now, Bruce, if you'll find a comfortable seat for you and Elaine, I'll bring out the records I have. I had everything of importance sent to me here."

Bruce rose, pulling out Elaine's chair for her, resting a large palm on her shoulder for an instant. "We're ready," he said. "I believe Elaine has an accurate picture of what's due in recent bills."

Beth had remained seated, leaning back in her chair and staring from one to the other of the three, her cheeks suddenly splotched with red. Then she sat forward with a thump and burst into speech.

"You're really going to go through with this, aren't you?" she demanded, looking at Al. "Right here and now you're going to discuss Frank's affairs with these strangers! You cold bastard!"

Shocked into stillness, Elaine stared from Beth's furious, contorted face to Al, tense as a drawn bow, his lanky body rigid.

"Strangers?" Al stuttered. "What in hell do you mean, Beth? Elaine was his *wife.*"

"Not for the past two years, she wasn't!" Beth shrieked. "Look at her!

Does she look like she's grieving? All she wants is to find out what she's getting." Her face swung to Elaine, her mouth working. "Well, I can tell you that! Frank left everything he had to you, *Mrs.* Jeffrey! And . . . and since you got a lawyer for yourself, just take the damned papers and go! You don't need any help from Al, and he knows it."

Somehow, Bruce's big hand was wrapped around Elaine's shaking fingers, hidden between them. He looked at Al, who was white as a sheet. "If that's true, Al," he said, his deep voice even, "I'll be glad to take over — unless you have some reason to go on with it."

Al shook his head, turning his back on his wife, walking toward Bruce and Elaine, his arms touching them lightly, herding them away from the table. There were tears of rage in his pale eyes. "You'll have to excuse Beth," he murmured, choked. "As you can see, she's drunk as hell. And very upset." He kept on talking, leading them toward the door. "Please try to understand, she's a very emotional woman. We were always so . . . so close to Frank. Like family.

She has the idea nobody cares." He was getting their coats, helping them on with them. "I was a fool to try this," he added, somewhat calmer. "We'll meet at your house, Elaine." He patted her shoulder, opening the door. "Please accept my apologies for my wife."

In the car, Elaine drew a long, shuddering breath and wrapped her coat around her. "What did you make of that?"

"She was drunk," Bruce said grimly, fitting the key into the ignition, "but she was probably right about part of it. Unless there's something more complicated than we've heard, we don't need Al." He switched on the lights as he waited for the heavy engine to warm up, and in the bluish glow from the dash his dark face was somber and thoughtful. He looked, Elaine thought, like the stranger Beth had called him. His outline in the modish, tailored clothes was so different; his shagginess was gone. A twinge of longing went through her for the burly man in the plaid shirt and jeans. She looked away, more lonely than ever.

"He means to be part of it, though."

"Yes, he does," Bruce said, still grim. "It will be interesting to find out why." He put the wagon in gear and started down the drive. "I hope you won't mind," he said in a different tone, "that I've brought my luggage along. I thought I might as well move in."

Elaine turned and looked at him. *Move in?* She had braced herself for being alone tonight, and while she realized that he would stay for the meeting with Al, she had thought he'd be grateful for the chance to get back to his friends at the hunt club after being snowbound for three days. He'd been awfully quiet at times, and she'd thought he'd probably been bored. Oh, not with the lovemaking, but he didn't have to *live* with her to make love. In her experience, men liked to spend their leisure time with other men, playing cards, talking, planning a hunt.

"You don't have to stay," she said, puzzled. "You've done enough for me."

The car swerved, then stopped with the headlights reflecting on glistening snow piled along the street. Bruce's arms caught her and yanked her close. "I'm

118

not doing it for you," he said roughly. "I'm doing it for me." His mouth closed over hers, as rough as his voice, then softened into a demanding passion as she yielded to him. It was a long kiss, finally ending with his face against her neck, his hand beneath her coat, hot and possessive on the thin silk. "Haven't you figured it out yet, Elaine? His voice was muffled and uneven, his breath warm on her skin. "I want to be with you as much as I can."

He was aching to go on, to tell her he loved her, that he wanted her whole future. Any other woman, he thought, would have known. But Elaine seemed insulated by her problems, living only in the present. She was warm, now, giving, her soft mouth searching for his and he raised his head. He kissed her again, but lightly. "Humor me," he said, half smiling. "Tell me I can stay."

He was no longer a stranger, no matter what he was wearing. She hugged him, laughing. "I'd love it, darling. You can stay as long as you want to."

His dark brows arched, the brown eyes

gleamed in the faint light. "Until the last possible minute?"

"Absolutely."

"I'll keep that in mind," Bruce said, and put the car in gear.

6

"ELAINE?" At ten-thirty the next morning, Al Fenton's voice was a thin sound on the telephone, a trifle more high-pitched than usual with embarrassment.

"Yes?" her bare feet chilly on the stone floor of the foyer, Elaine did her best to sound impersonally pleasant.

"I'd like to meet with you and Bruce at your place this evening, if that suits you."

"That will be fine." It would be fine like a trip to the dentist, but it had to be done. "What time shall I tell Bruce?"

"Let's make it early — it may be a long session. How would seven o'clock agree with your plans? Oh, and before I forget again, I wanted to ask you what to do with Frank's car. He — that is, we rode together that day. The car's here, parked with mine in our garage. I could drive it up this evening and leave it there, then come back down with Bruce."

Elaine's thoughts reeled. How stupid she had been — of course Frank would have had a car, and she'd never even wondered about it. "Don't bother," she said, knowing she wouldn't want the car around. "I'll have it picked up and put in storage, Al. When everything is straightened out, I imagine the best thing to do will be to sell it."

"I'm not sure of that." Al's voice grew stronger. "You might like to keep it. It's almost new, one of those little two-seater Mercedes. Blue and white, classy. Beth loves it."

Anger rose in Elaine's throat. No matter how often she insisted she wanted nothing that had been Frank's, no one believed her. "Not my style," she said flatly. "Let's sell it. At seven this evening, then. I'll tell Bruce."

"Wait," Al said hastily, hearing the finality in her tone. "Beth wants to speak to you." He put the phone down and Elaine could hear footsteps, murmuring voices. Then one voice: Beth's.

"Elaine? I simply wanted to apologize. There was no excuse for the way I acted last night. Those martinis . . . " She gave an exaggerated groan. "Really, I ought to leave them alone! Actually, I barely remember what went on, but Al has very kindly filled me in on all the idiotic things I said. I hope you didn't take me seriously. And do tell Bruce I regret my behavior, will you?"

"Of course," Elaine answered pleasantly, "and think no more about it, Beth. We all have our moments."

Hanging up, Elaine grimaced. The apology had been delivered in such a pleasant, offhand way, touched with casual humor. The kind of social skill she remembered from the wives of Frank's friends. Under the pretense, Beth had really been saying that she wasn't sorry at all, but she did have good manners. And, Elaine admitted to herself as she went in search of Bruce, her own reply was just as transparent — *I don't believe you, but my manners are good, too.*

Entering the big room, Elaine's bare feet made no sound. She stopped, catching sight of Bruce standing at the gun cabinet across the room and feeling the silly little thump in her heart that was becoming familiar. Bruce was wearing jeans and a thick chamois-colored wool shirt that made his black hair blacker, his shoulders even broader. Elaine had a sudden unwelcome vision of what it would have been like if he had gone back to the club to stay. The big room empty, cold even with the fire . . . She shook off the fancy and went toward him.

"Beth Fenton wants you to know she regrets her behavior," she said as he turned, "and Al Fenton wants to confer with us both this evening, beginning at seven."

Bruce's eyes went over her, remembering. By chance, Elaine had put on the same light slacks and pale green cotton-knit pullover she had been wearing the day they met, and as usual the wide neckline had slipped to one side, exposing a delicate shoulder that he now knew was as satin-smooth as it looked. He reached out, putting a long arm around her waist and drawing her against his side, looking down into those impractically big eyes. "And what is it *you* want?"

Elaine laughed, leaning into the big, warm body, dropping her forehead against him. The laughter was directed mostly at herself. They had made love less than an hour ago, going back to bed again after breakfast. Yet here she was, with a flood of warmth coiling temptingly in her loins at his touch. "I'd never dare tell you," she said, swallowing the rest of the laughter. "You'd think I was crazy." She pulled away, still smiling, and looked at the open doors of the cabinet. "What are you doing? Checking out the weapons? They'll be yours, you know. They go with the house."

Bruce looked at her incredulously. "I do think you're crazy, love. There's a small fortune here. See those two in the middle? Both of them are handmade, British built. Worth at least six thousand for the rifle, probably eight for the shotgun. And the one off to the side by itself is an antique, a rare one. I'd say the whole collection plus the cabinet, would bring at least twenty, maybe thirty thousand dollars." He reached in, straightening one of the shotguns, frowning a little. "This one, however, could use a good cleaning. Careless to put it back without at least wiping it down." He stood staring critically at the dull barrel until his attention was caught by the silence, by the absolute stillness of Elaine's slender figure beside him. He turned and looked down at her, at the shocked horror, the sick guilt in her silvery eyes.

"Oh, my God . . . " he uttered, and put his arms around her, pressing her face into his shoulder. "It can't be the same gun, Elaine. Who would bring it back here?" Inside, he was cursing himself for stupidity, for an absolute lack of common sense. It probably was the same gun. The rack had been custom built for the collection, each padded niche the right depth and length for the varying sizes, and there were no empty spaces. Still holding her, he pushed the doors closed with a booted toe, feeling her try to breathe deeply, her breasts heaving against him.

"I'm all right," she said, her breath catching and then steadying. "I really am." She drew away a little. "It was just seeing it and then suddenly remembering how lethal a shotgun is at . . . at close range." She looked up at him, her soft mouth twisting. "How could he? How

126

could anyone who knew what would happen possibly pull the trigger?"

"He *didn't*! Dammitall! It was an *accident*!" Shocked by his own sudden, deep roar, Bruce swept her up violently and stalked to the other end of the room. "I'm sorry," he growled, "I shouldn't have yelled at you. But dammit, Elaine, whether he did or he didn't, no matter what happened, it wasn't your fault!" He sank down in the big chair, still holding her, studying her startled face. "All right," he said, more gently, "I made a lot of noise. But I don't want you hurting, love. I want you happy."

She relaxed, settling into his embrace. His noise and violence had shocked her completely out of her sick imaginings. "I am happy," she said, sounding faintly surprised. "I don't think about any of it very often, now. Mostly, I'm very happy, being with you."

Bruce looked at her silently, his arms tightening. "That's good news," he said after a moment. "Do you think it might last?"

She smiled and put an arm around his neck, pulling him down and kissing him

127

sensuously, loving the feel of his warm mouth and soft beard. "Long enough to get us through this," she said, "if we don't get too much interference from the Fentons. And long enough that I already know I'll never forget you." For a moment, she was lost in the depths of those soft brown eyes, and then her own eyes clouded. She slid quickly from his lap, stretching and looking into the fire.

"Let's do something," she suggested. "Take a walk, go for a ride — something. I need to get out, don't you?"

He knew she'd slipped away again, cautious and wary. Somehow any hint of permanence frightened her. "Sure," he said casually, "it sounds great. But you'd better put on some warmer clothes."

Running lightly up the stairs, Elaine headed for her room with her thin eyebrows knitted, her throat aching. Her imagination was working entirely too well today. She had just seen herself back in her apartment in South Carolina, trying to forget the man she had just said she would never forget. Damn. It had taken two years to put together a reasonable facsimile of an independent female, and here she was, mooning miserably about being without him. Leaving Frank had been like bursting out into sunlight, into a fresh new world. But leaving Bruce?

Don't think about it, she told herself, thrusting her slender legs into heavy jeans, then grabbing a thick jacket. *When the time comes, you'll go.* This was the same world Frank had, wealth and sports, insincere men, catty women. Bruce was nothing like Frank, but it was clear that he fit in here. She didn't. And she didn't want to, either.

They drove, up steep and rocky roads, until the roads ended. Then they walked, through trails Bruce knew, following frozen streams to narrow but sheer waterfalls that refused to freeze, the frigid water slipping from under ice above, past dripping icicles to fall in pools and disappear under the ice again. Then they walked farther, Elaine following Bruce's long, tireless stride with panting determination. The snow in the open was almost gone, melting away in slow rivulets under the sun. They stood on high places and looked out over smaller peaks and valleys without end, and Bruce pointed out to her the hillside where his family had lived. His father, he said, had farmed the small valley that lay below it; his mother had taught in the village school.

"You've come a long way," she commented, and watched his slow, reminiscent smile.

"I make more money than my father did," he said, "but I'm no better a man. I'm still proud to be his son."

She liked that remark. When they started down again, she put her hand in his and held on, slipping and sliding and utterly out of breath when they reached the wagon. Bruce looked at his watch and frowned.

"It's later than I thought. We'll have to have a quick dinner if we're going to be ready for Al at seven. Let's hope we get it over with tonight."

Elaine was amazed at how far and how fast her heart sank at his words. She climbed into the wagon, leaned back, and gave herself a short lecture. Of course he wanted this to end. She knew he called his office in Atlanta often and carried on long discussions. But it was understandable that the delay in his return would cause problems.

"I need to get back, too," she said, following the logical course of her thoughts. "I'd like to find a job before the holidays start."

Bruce was backing to turn, his head twisted to look behind him. "Don't make any plans," he said over his shoulder. "There's a lot to do after we talk to Al. We'll want to put the will through probate in Atlanta, and you know how long that can take."

"No, I don't," Elaine said, somewhat crossly. "I don't even know what probate is. But however long it takes, I expect I'll think it's too long."

As he straightened the car, his face came back around with a wicked grin. "It can't take too long to suit me. I'll have you where I want you."

Elaine flushed. "I would bet," she said threateningly, hanging on as they started down the rough road, "that I could take that will to any court in Georgia."

Bruce was silent, watching the deep holes and maneuvering past boulders. When they reached a smoother section of graveled road, he glanced over at her. "For some reason," he said softly, "I thought you might want to be with me."

Elaine took her gaze away from his brown velvet eyes with some difficulty and concentrated on the sheer rock faces and bleak winter woods they were passing. "You know I do," she said finally. "I want to be with you until that last possible minute. We'll make it Atlanta."

Bruce let out his breath, slowly and silently, his eyes fixed on the road. "That's better," he said, though her answer hadn't satisfied him at all. He went right on thinking about what she had implied. In the beginning, he had thought she shied away from commitment simply because they barely knew each other. Now he was becoming convinced that she had at least considered a future together and had turned it down. He was a man accustomed to marshaling all the facts, no matter how hidden, before he took a case to court. She trusted him; he knew that. And in bed she gave him more passion than he had thought her small body could hold. And he knew she liked him. But maybe that was all; maybe it would always be all. His hands tightened on the wheel, remembering that she married once without love; very possibly, she didn't want to do it again. His brown eyes grew as bleak as the scenes around him as he thought back about his own life. There had been several women he had trusted, had enjoyed sex with, and had liked very well. He had never considered marrying them. So how could he blame her? Maybe the evidence was all in and he'd lost the case.

"Bruce?"

He glanced over, seeing the small, fine-boned face still pink from exercise, the enormous light gray eyes fixed on his face. They were running free on a smoothly paved road now, nearing the turn that led to the house, and he sat back, relaxing, smiling at her.

"What's up? You look worried."

"What I am is scared," Elaine said, "and I don't know why. I keep thinking Al Fenton is going to spring something on us that we won't like."

"If he does," Bruce said, far more cheerfully than he felt, "I'll stomp on him."

She gave a small, surprised ripple of laughter and slid across the seat, curling against him, her hand resting lightly on his thigh. "You make it sound so simple."

Bruce laughed and put an arm around her. "Whatever, I'll take care of it. Don't worry." He felt her relax, her head dropping on his shoulder, heard her relieved sigh. His arm tightened. This case wasn't over, the jury was still out, and he might win yet.

* * *

Elaine was still stacking dishes in the dishwasher, still wearing her jeans and loose shirt, when she heard Bruce answer the door and then the blending of his deep voice with Al's high, penetrating tone. The voices fades, and she knew Bruce had taken Al into the room they never used, the dining room on the other side of the foyer. The big table there, and the overhead chandelier, made a more convenient place for a meeting.

She punched the dishwasher on and ran upstairs to brush her hair and put it up properly. The clothes would do, she thought. If Al wanted to look at a fashionably dressed woman, he could go home and look at his wife.

Al had taken the contents from a briefcase and spread them on the table before she entered. Elaine glanced at them and then sat down. Bruce pulled out a chair beside her, and Al, his smile fixed in place, sat down across from them.

"Bruce tells me you two have been hiking the mountaintops all afternoon," he said pleasantly. "I envy you. I need exercise myself. I haven't been out since . . . well, for sometime."

Elaine knew what the hesitation and change of phrase meant, and wondered if Al was trying to remind her of that tragic afternoon. But she nodded and smiled and said something agreeable, turning her attention to Bruce. He had picked up the copy of Frank's will and was reading it. She saw his eyes sharpen once and then go on, his face impassive.

It seemed a remarkably short time before he laid it down.

"I see nothing difficult," he said to Al. "Elaine as executrix and sole beneficiary could hardly be simpler. But I do find it unusual that Jeffrey didn't mention any assets or properties. Not even this house, though the will was signed only four months ago."

The smile remained pasted on Al's long face. "Frank made no investments. In spite of my advice and arguments, he preferred to keep his money fluid and spend it freely. As for properties, he never kept anything very long. A very restless man. Bought and sold and moved continually, both here and abroad. Knowing his habits, it seemed unnecessary to burden the document with a house that would be probably be sold in a year. He knew I'd keep up with things. I've handled his finances for years, and I can tell you he never knew or cared about what he owned or owed."

"Risky," Bruce said dryly. "What if something had happened to you first?"

Al's nostrils flared. "I do have partners," he said stiffly. "I think you could trust

Harrison and Toth to come up with the figures."

"Then you handled it all through the firm?"

Al colored. "Naturally. I met Frank through my father-in-law, John Harrison, who turned Frank's account over to me. We became friends immediately, and it's been a close relationship."

Bruce stared at him meditatively. "I believe," he said finally, "that you told Elaine you had some surprises. Let's hear them."

Al shuffled through the papers and handed Bruce a sheaf of what appeared to be statements. "I think Elaine is aware of the biggest problem, and she's probably told you," he said. "Frank died penniless. And in debt. Deeply in debt."

Elaine, who had been thinking that Al Fenton had a bad habit of making things sound overly dramatic, spoke up impatiently. "The house will take care of the debts."

Fenton leaned back, looking uncomfortable. "I'm afraid not. Elaine. Not even if you sold it at its full value,

137

and certainly not at what you and Bruce have agreed on as a price." He looked at Bruce's suddenly curious face and added, "I asked Paul Somers about it. I'd heard talk it was under market, and it certainly was." His tone had become very critical.

"I set the price," Elaine said coolly, "at the amount it took to pay the bills."

"I'm sorry," Al said, "truly sorry I let you make that mistake. If I'd had any idea you would hurry into decisions without my advice, I would have talked to you earlier. The truth of the matter is that Frank owed another hundred and fifty thousand. To me." He reached into the pile of papers and extracted one, sliding it over to Bruce. "His personal note, signed on the same day as his will, you can see."

Elaine, staring at Fenton's long face, was trying to get her breath. She had no doubt he was telling the truth; he wouldn't have handed that paper to Bruce so carelessly if it weren't authentic. "Good Lord," she said, subdued, "I'll never be able to pay off everything."

Fenton smiled suddenly. "No problem.

That's the other surprise. You'll have more than enough. There's an insurance policy — "

"Just a minute," Bruce interrupted, frowning. "If you were handling Jeffrey's finances, then you knew he couldn't repay the loan. Why did you give him the money?"

Watching, Elaine was sure Al had expected the question. He spread his hands and shrugged. "We were friends," he said. "What could I do? I'd been warning him for years, showing him statements, begging him to settle down. He wouldn't even look at them; he just laughed and said the money would last his lifetime." He sat forward, running a hand over his narrow chin, hiding his mouth. "Besides, he'd finished the house and I thought I might get the money back when he sold. In any event, I couldn't bring myself to refuse."

If it was an act, Elaine thought, it was a good one. Al had certainly given an accurate picture of Frank's attitude toward money. And of course the hundred and fifty thousand probably wasn't a huge sum to the Fentons. She looked at Bruce, seeing his dark face solemn but still impassive, giving no hint to his thoughts. She reached over and took the paper, studying it. Properly signed and notarized, and, to give Al credit, at a very low interest rate. She handed it back to him, wondering how in the world she would ever clear up Frank's debts. The car would bring a little . . . She turned and looked at Al again.

"You mentioned an insurance policy that might help," she said, keeping her voice even. "Tell us about it."

"It won't just help," Fenton said, "it will take care of everything. Frank's father took it out thirty years ago, and, thank God, it's paid up." He picked up a blue folder and took out a bound set of yellowed pages, automatically handing them to Bruce. "It was an annuity," Al said to Elaine. "In a few years, it would have begun paying him a small income. However, it's also a life-insurance policy, and it's a big one. Two hundred and fifty thousand." His pale eyes went from Elaine's startled face to Bruce's lifted brows and back again. "I thought you might have known about it, Elaine, until I saw how worried you were about his debts. There's also double indemnity for an accidental death. So, since it's made out with Frank's estate as beneficiary, the estate will benefit by a half million." He leaned back and smiled at them both as if he alone had been responsible for an incredible stroke of good luck.

Bruce's gaze shot to Elaine's stricken face. If he knew anything about this woman and her stubborn idealism, she was about to set Al Fenton on his ear.

Elaine was struggling only to find the right words. Al seemed to feel bad enough about losing a friend, without adding to his grief by letting him know what she was sure had really happened. But it had to be said, some way.

"No," she got out, "that can't happen. We can't take the double indemnity, Al. Frank's death wasn't accidental. I . . . I have proof it wasn't."

For a long moment, Al simply stared at Elaine, and then he was struggling to his feet, knocking over a chair that fell on the floor with a resounding crash. "Good God!" he burst out. "Of course it was an accident! Frank Jeffrey didn't have an enemy in the world!" Al's face was greenish-white, his mouth shaking. "What in the hell do you mean, *proof*? You couldn't have proof . . . "

Shocked, Elaine was trying to explain. "Wait, Al . . . maybe it isn't legal proof, but I don't think you know what I meant . . . "

Fury flared behind the pale eyes staring at her. "I don't think you know what you're asking for, either!" Al snapped out. "When you start crying murder, you'd better remember where *you* were that day. I know you sneaked into town that morning, and I know you were out at that farm at just about the right time! The sheriff told me — " His voice was cut off abruptly as Bruce's hand shot across the table and clutched him by the throat.

"That's enough!" Dragging the struggling Fenton around the corner of the table, Bruce shoved him into another chair and stood over him. Fenton was no match for Bruce, and he evidently knew it. He huddled there, trying to catch his breath, his whole body shaking. Elaine could see Bruce gradually controlling his own temper.

"You damned fool!" Bruce growled finally, his deep voice utterly disgusted. "Elaine didn't think Frank was murdered. She believes he committed suicide."

Panting, rubbing his bruised neck, Fenton looked up at Bruce with a mixture of fear and incredulity on his white face. "Suicide? On a barbed-wire fence?"

Bruce let out his breath in an impatient grunt. He could hardly blame Fenton for that stupid question. It had been his own first reaction, too. "To make it look accidental," he said tiredly, and turned and looked at Elaine. He wished he could put his arms around her and comfort her. She was pale and distressed, her huge eyes shadowed, her lips trembling.

"You'd better go get that note," he said gently, "or Al is going to think you're out of your mind."

Elaine nodded quickly and got up, glad to have a purpose. She turned at the door and looked back at Bruce's grim face. "I'm sorry," she said hesitantly. "I had to say it."

143

The faintest of smiles parted Bruce's black beard. "I knew you would. It's all right."

She went on, even more shaken by that smile, by the way he understood. She couldn't believe any man could know her feelings as well as Bruce did. She had not only disrupted the meeting, spoiled Al's plan, but also she'd done it so badly that Bruce had had to intervene physically. Yet he wasn't angry with her, only with that idiot Fenton, who had practically accused her of murder. She shuddered, running up the stairs to the drawer where she kept the note. Both of the Fentons had evidently let their loyalty to Frank persuade them that the woman who had left him must be a monster.

Fenton was sitting up straight in his chair when she returned. He had smoothed his hair and attempted to set his tie and rumpled collar into place. "I humbly apologize," he said as she handed him the note. "I know I'm entirely too emotional about Frank's death. But I honestly did wonder why you had come to town and why you'd gone out to the farm. The sheriff said you'd been there

144

so close to the time of death that it was a mercy you hadn't seen it. Bruce has just explained why you came and why you were looking for Frank. I really am sorry."

"I can see that," Elaine answered. She truly could. "I hadn't thought of it, Al. The trip over was a failure, anyway . . . " Her voice wavered, and Bruce pulled out a chair for her. She sat, touching his hand lightly as he slid in beside her, hoping the touch would tell him how glad she was he was here. This meeting would have been horrible without him. She looked at Al, who was bent over the note, and thought how serious he looked.

"This isn't proof of intention," Al said slowly, "yet I can see how it would have worried you." He laid the note down on the table but kept on staring at it, muscles moving jerkily along his thin jaw. "I think it would have upset me, too, Elaine."

Elaine glanced at Bruce, catching a quizzical look in his brown eyes. He leaned forward, closer to Al. "You knew Jeffrey better than almost anyone, Al. Do you really think he was the kind who would kill himself?"

Al folded the note nervously and pushed it aside. "If he did," he said with an effort, "he would probably have done it just that way. He'd hide it. He wouldn't have wanted anyone to know." He shook his head sadly. "Poor guy. How he must have felt."

"Wait a minute," Bruce said harshly. "Now you sound as if you believe he *did* take his own life! Why didn't you suspect it before?"

Al flushed, blotches of red appearing in his white cheeks. "Well, hell, Bruce — I thought it was an accident. I hadn't seen this note, remember. And while I knew Frank was upset, I didn't think things were that bad with him."

"But he was upset?"

"Naturally. Money was as necessary to Frank as oxygen, and he was fast running out of it."

Bruce sighed, his hand covering Elaine's under the table, pressing it warmly. He knew what this was doing to her. "Then," he went on to Al, "if you think it's a real possibility, what do you think we should do about it?"

146

Al leaned back, his hands clasped together on the table in an effort to control his still-shaky fingers. "I'd strongly advise you to leave it alone. The death is officially recorded as an accident, and both the sheriff and his deputy viewed the body at the scene. It would be damned hard to change their testimony. As for the note, Bruce, you and I both know a judge would never take it seriously. There are no facts in it. Just suggestions that could mean anything."

Elaine's eyes went back and forth between the two men, seeing the tacit admission in Bruce's eyes that Al was right.

"But if we don't mention it," she said, "won't we be cheating the insurance company?"

"*If* it was suicide," Fenton said. "Try to remember, Elaine, that we don't know and never will know that it wasn't an accident. But even if it was, *we* aren't cheating them — Frank did. And he had a reason besides his pride. That policy has a suicide clause. They'd pay nothing if they could prove he killed himself. He knew what he owed — maybe he wanted

147

to be sure it was paid." He paused to let that sink in, and then went on: "Put it out of your mind. Take the money and pay his debts, and then, if you don't want to keep the rest of it, give it to charity. But for godsake, don't start a lot of useless talk. Let Frank rest in peace."

"Very sensible," Bruce said, rising. He ignored Elaine's desperate look and began putting the papers together. "I'm sure you're right, Al. The law can't be changed by opinions, only facts. And there are no facts to prove suicide." Keeping the will and the insurance policy to one side, he put the rest of the records into Al's briefcase. Taking it, Al hesitated, looking at the will and the policy still on the table.

"I can take care of those, too," he said to Elaine. "I'm familiar with Frank's problems. Why not just turn the paperwork over to me? Bruce has his own legal firm to run, and I expect he'd like to get back to it."

Moving between Al and Elaine, Bruce clapped a hand on Al's shoulder. "Don't you want me to earn my fee, Al? I may be a week or so getting that will through probate, but I'll let you know as soon as I do. And I'll notify the insurance company."

"All right." Al stood up, giving Elaine a rueful smile and offering Bruce his hand. "I never thought I'd thank someone for choking me, Bruce, but I think I should. I'd already said too much."

"Yes, you had." Bruce's eyes glinted as he took the hand. "But I think we all have a better idea of the situation now. The air is cleared."

Feeling bruised and forlorn, Elaine still sat at the long table as Bruce took Fenton to the door and bid him goodnight. She supposed that everything they had decided was both logical and inevitable and that she had been impossibly idealistic. But she was so positive. Even without the note, it would have been hard to believe that Frank could have done such a stupid, dangerous thing. He did take sports seriously, and he knew about guns. He had often spoken in disgust about hunters who were careless. She stood up as Bruce came in and went toward him.

"I've been thinking . . . "

"Too much," Bruce supplied. "The past is over." He scooped up the two documents from the table and put them in a drawer of the big buffet. Coming back to her, he put his big hands on her shoulders, looking in to her eyes.

"I *know* how you feel, darling. And I'm not letting the matter drop. But there's absolutely no use in talking to Al about it. His feelings are set, he has reasons of his own. And he's *out*, as of now."

"Oh." Elaine relaxed, drawing a deep breath. "Then you're going to look into it further yourself?"

"I am," Bruce said firmly. "And when I get through, you're going to be free of every doubt. But this has been a long and miserable session, and we're going to forget it now. We aren't going to talk about it; we aren't even going to think about it."

Elaine smiled wistfully. "That doesn't sound easy."

"On the contrary," Bruce said, turning her briskly toward the door, "it's going to be a piece of cake. First, as a

150

symbolic gesture of ridding ourselves of the evening, we're going to take a shower. Together. We don't get out until we're sure there isn't a thought in our head. Then, concentrating on a contest I've just invented . . . "

Elaine began to laugh. "What contest?"

They were in the foyer, heading toward the stairs. Bruce stopped, raising his eyebrows at her. "Why, a contest as to which one of us will first drive the other one mad with desire. What else?"

Elaine choked down her laughter and gave him a considering look. "Best two out of three?"

"Oh, Lord," Bruce said, picking her up, "you do drive a hard bargain. But I'll try." He slung her slender body over one shoulder and started up the stairs, two steps at a time.

7

IN the dim room, the outlines of the heavy furniture were just visible in the first faint light before dawn. It was quiet and warm, and Elaine was conscious of comfort and a fleeting dream, but also of a tickling sensation on her back and murmuring in her ear. She yawned and opened her eyes.

"Hmm?"

"I asked you," Bruce said with dignity, "if you'd like to try for three out of three."

She groaned and turned, flinging herself against him, her hair spraying over his face, her own face buried somewhere in his shoulder. "You rat," she mumbled. "I was still *sleeping*. And, besides, it isn't even daylight."

He fastened his big body around her like an octopus, arms and legs wrapped and twined. "But, angel, you did so well last night. Drove me out of my mind twice in a row. I thought it was only fair to offer you a chance at a tournament sweep. Sort of a grand slam?"

Elaine giggled, in spite of herself and then yawned again, settling into his embrace. He did feel good. The springy hairs on his chest were like tiny flowers, caressing her breasts. "Mmm." Her eyes kept closing, the heavy lids dropping like curtains. "After breakfast?"

There was a short silence. "Can't," Bruce said finally. "I'm leaving."

She shot up in a sitting position, brushed her hair back with both hands, and stared at him. "*Leaving?*"

Bruce grinned. "If I wanted to wake you up, I guess I hit on the right words." His eyes were teasing, growing very warm as they ran over her.

Elaine was embarrassed, realizing all at once how she'd given herself away. Possessive. Damn. Men didn't like possessive women. "I'm sorry," she said, averting her gaze, noticing her nakedness and pulling up a corner of the sheet to cover herself. "Naturally, you have to get back to your office sometime. I was just surprised."

"And I was flattered." He drew her

back down beside him again and began stroking slowly along her gleaming curves and hollows. His hand flattened warmly on the ivory silk of her belly and made circles around the small navel, then digressed, inventing tender forays with one finger along the soft creases of her loins. "Now," he added softly, "how about that three out of three? Or do you concede that it's my turn to drive you mad with desire?"

Her eyes closed, her lips slightly parted, Elaine had gone boneless in his arms, completely relaxed. "From the way I feel," she murmured, "it must be your turn." She felt the soft beard touch her breast, the tongue curl around the tip and tug, and then drew in her breath as his hand slowly became more intimate. "Oh-h-h, Bruce . . . "

Amazed as always at how quickly her passion rose to meet his, Bruce still took his time, his hands and bearded face exploring her, his hard, heated loins pressing against her until they were both trembling. Finally, when she could stand it no longer, she wrapped her slender legs around him and demanded that he take her.

"Now," she whispered fiercely. "Now . . . " And then, shuddering with pleasure as he entered her, sliding firmly into the cradle of her thighs until they were knitted tightly together, she opened her eyes and looked down at their joined bodies. "Ah, Bruce . . . it's wonderful." her voice trembled, her eyes swept up to his. "How I'm going to hate that last possible minute."

He gathered her to him, his hands slipping beneath her rounded hips to begin again to reach for ultimate pleasure. He could have told her that the last possible minute was a lifetime away. Because at this moment, for the first time, he believed it. She was going to love him.

★ ★ ★

"Maybe two days, maybe even three," Bruce said after breakfast. "I wish you'd go with me. You can stay in my apartment, and Atlanta isn't at all bad in the winter." He was dressed in a different but still impressive suit, gray flannel, with a white shirt and a black and gray tie. Not a diplomat this time, Elaine decided, brooding over him with fond eyes. A stockbroker, maybe. Conservative, trustworthy.

"I'll stay here," she said, "and keep the home fires burning." She smiled at him and then looked serious. "Is there anything I should be doing about — well, about anything?"

Bruce winced. "Please don't try. Stay as far away from Al Fenton as you can. I'll stop in town and sign that contract for the house with Paul Somers, which will be pending the probate, naturally, and the title search."

Elaine nodded. She had no idea what he meant, but she was sure it was right. She followed him out to the foyer and helped him into his coat, struggling with a sharp pang of premature loneliness. When he turned to kiss her good-bye, she was smiling brightly with tears in her eyes.

"Hey!" Bruce said unevenly. "None of that." Cupping her head in his hands, he kissed the tears away. "I'm coming right back, dammit." Then he kissed the smile, a properly improper kiss. She clung to him for a moment, breathing in the scent of wool, of soap, of warm male skin, storing it up. Then she stepped away.

"Hey!" she said imitating him. "Don't worry about me. I even cry at movies. Have a safe trip."

Bruce was dazzled by the look in her eyes. Something tender had emerged, shining but soft as a misty dawn. He strode determinedly toward the garage, hurrying now. He had a feeling he was entering a damned prickly thicket after promising her he'd free her of her doubts. Because if what he suspected was true, it made it a lot less likely that Frank Jeffrey's death had been accidental, and that was something he did not want to tell Elaine.

★ ★ ★

Shortly after noon, a small station wagon drove into the parking area of the house and stopped. Elaine had been practicing preventive medicine against an attack of depression, cleaning furiously in the big room. She had dusted and vacuumed and was beginning on the glass wall when she heard the car and went to the window. A short, compact man was climbing out of the wagon and walking briskly toward the front door. Paul Somers — probably here to talk to Bruce about the sale. Elaine went quickly to let him in. She had met Somers only twice, once when she'd gone to his office and once when he came to appraise the house, but she liked him. He was friendly and down to earth and they'd been on a first-name basis almost immediately. In fact, she thought now, Paul and Carl Hanley, the sheriff, had seemed like her kind of people, honest and open.

Paul came in smiling, whipping a knitted cap from his tight-curled sandy hair and struggling out of a down-filled jacket. "Bruce was in," he said, "and I wish I had more clients like him. He laid a hefty sum on me and said we could have the rest when we needed it." His hazel eyes twinkled. "I do like a generous man."

Elaine laughed and took his coat and cap, hanging them up. "There's a fire in the fireplace," she said, "and I'll make some coffee. I could use a cup myself." She was glad to have company.

Paul followed her to the kitchen, leaning against the door jamb and surveying the wild colors while she worked. He was so used to appraising houses that his eyes were always wandering, judging. "What did Bruce think of this kitchen?"

Elaine's look of surprise was quite visible. "I don't think he ever mentioned it, Paul. Why? Did he say anything to you?"

Paul laughed. "No. But I've known Bruce a long time, and he's pretty conservative. This looks like an explosion in a Mexican paint factory."

She giggled. "Yes, it does. But it's the latest thing, I guess. And it's easy to change, except for the tile." She handed him a brimming cup and went with him back to the fire. Sitting down, Paul made a casual remark about solid comfort and then got straight to the point.

"Elaine, did you know you owned this house?"

"I know it was left to me," she said,

puzzled. "But Bruce said it couldn't be sold until the will was probated."

"Yeah, but that was probably because he thought the same thing I did — that Jeffrey owned it. But something made him wonder, I guess, because when he came in this morning, he asked me if I'd checked the county records when I listed it. I hadn't, because I'd handled the sale of the land, the house is new, and I figured there wouldn't be much of a title search. But after he left, I got curious and went over to check. The house is in your name. Jeffrey signed it over to you a couple of months ago."

Amazed, Elaine looked at Somers with disbelief. "Could he do that without my permission?"

Paul laughed a little. "Sure. There's no law that says you can't give something away. You'd have found it out when the taxes came due."

"But . . . " The sick feeling of guilt crawled inexorably into Elaine's stomach. The only reason she could think of for Frank to sign away his new house was because he had known he wasn't going to need it. Had he been planning to

160

kill himself that long? Two months? She swallowed against the nausea. "Does Bruce know?"

"I think he does now. The clerk at records said another man had just been in checking the same property, and from her description it sounded like Bruce." Paul sipped his coffee, looking thoughtfully at Elaine. "I didn't mean to upset you. I know it's crazy, but it's legal. What I wanted to point out is that you don't have to wait. If you want the sale to go through right away, we can arrange it."

She shook her head. "I don't know — I'll talk to Bruce." She felt sad and confused, wishing Bruce were there right now. Trying a smile, she added, "He's representing me in settling the estate."

Paul smiled back at her, finishing his coffee. "Good. I was afraid you'd get stuck with Al Fenton. Maybe I'm prejudiced, but I can't stand that particular bunch from Atlanta. Too slick."

Elaine smiled this time in spite of her feelings. "Bruce is from Atlanta," she pointed out, half teasing. "He's one of the same crowd."

"Don't kid yourself," Paul said, grinning.

"He went to Atlanta and made it big, I'll admit. But he's not one of them, he's one of us." He put down his cup and rose. "You just let me know when Bruce comes back and we'll set up a closing date. If you're like most people, you can use the money."

Elaine maintained an easy manner as she saw Paul out, but as he drove away she could feel the guilt returning. Doggedly, she went back to cleaning the glass doors, telling herself not to be morbid, not to consider it proof. She knew a judge would pay no more attention to a man signing his house over to his wife than he would to the note. There just *was* no proof! When she thought about it sensibly, she felt Bruce's continuing investigation was nothing but a waste of time. But she was still grateful to him for trying.

By afternoon the next day, the whole house inside was shining clean. Restless still, Elaine showered, dressed in plain black wool slacks and a sweater, threw on her fur lined cape, and went into the little town. The weather had moderated, the roads were clear of ice, and her car was safe, even with the slightly worn tires. She spent an hour or so wandering in and out of the small stores, looking at woodcrafts and handwoven rugs and hangings. Then she shopped in earnest at the grocery, buying a bagful of fresh vegetables, milk, and butter. She was carrying them out when Beth Fenton hailed her from the other side of the street. Elaine stopped, clutching the bag in both arms, and waited for Beth to cross and come up to her. Beth eyed her burden with amusement.

"Couldn't you find someone to deliver that?" she asked lightly. "I want to talk to you. Is there somewhere you can put it down?" Beth was dressed exquisitely in a soft blue suit and matching coat, her hair in a golden chignon under a tiny, brimmed hat, diamonds sparkling in her ears. On the dingy street she looked like a beautiful visitor from another planet. Elaine suddenly wondered why Beth had married Al Fenton. After all, it wasn't for money; she was the one who had that.

"The logical place to put it down," she answered cheerfully, "is in the back seat of my car. It's only a half block from here." She started off, leaving Beth to follow. The high heels tapped irritatingly along behind her. After Elaine deposited the bag in the car, she faced Beth with what she hoped was a pleasant smile. "What are we to talk about?"

Beth was staring at the little car, looking dismayed. "Al said you were planning on selling Frank's car — but, looking at this one . . . "

"I'm selling," Elaine said, inwardly amused. "Why?"

The greenish eyes looked relieved. "I want to buy it. I hear you're planning on having it picked up, stored, and then sold. If you have no objection to selling it to me, I'd like to have you leave it where it is."

"I'll be glad to sell it to you, and glad to leave it where it is," Elaine answered. "But Al seemed to want it moved. Have you talked to him?"

"He has nothing to do with it," Beth said flatly. "How much do you want for it?" She was opening her purse and pulling out a checkbook. "I'll take care of it right now."

"Wait." Elaine was both surprised and

confused. "It has to be appraised, and I can't sell it anyway, Beth, until the . . . the estate is settled." She watched the golden brows rise, the red lips open, then snap shut.

"But . . . well, I suppose that's right." For once, Beth seemed at a loss. She put the checkbook back in place and added, "You're sure? I mean, you will leave it with me?"

Was there a tinge of pleading in Beth's usually confident tone? "Certainly," Elaine said quickly, "if Al doesn't object."

"He won't." Beth started to turn away, then turned back again. "Al was very pleased at how smoothly things went at your meeting, by the way. He said there were no problems, and that Bruce was taking over the paperwork." Her eyes glinted again with superior amusement. "It must be nice to have someone like Bruce McClure running your little errands."

"He seems very efficient," Elaine said stiffly, getting into her car. The meeting went *smoothly*? Al hadn't given his wife the full story. She wondered how he had explained the bruises on his neck. Driving away, she looked in the rearview mirror and saw Beth across the street, getting into a small Mercedes, blue and white. She grinned wryly. So, she had taken possession already. Beth really wanted that car.

That evening, there was nothing left to do. Time stretched endlessly. It had been two days, so evidently it was going to be three. Elaine sat in the chair in front of the fire, with the other chair glaringly empty, and tried in vain to shore up her defenses. In the past two years, she had spent evening after evening alone and perfectly happy. She had read good books, listened to the stereo, and considered herself lucky. So, here there was a built-in stereo in a low cabinet on the fireplace wall, there were books, mostly new and unread, in a bookcase. She tried them both, settling back in the chair with a best seller she hadn't read, with soft background music to soothe her irritable feelings. In less than a half hour, she leaped from the chair, switched off the stereo, flung the book on the table and herself back into the chair, biting her lip and staring at the fire.

The worst of it was she knew what was happening to her. Or, rather *had* happened to her. The symptoms matched those described to her in the past by emotionally torn friends, and she had also read about them in dramatic novels. She had never really believed they happened to normal, non-neurotic people, but, dammit, here they were. She was physically aching for the sight of that big, bearded hunk, and the realization filled her with anger and despair. Loneliness she could understand, but not this actual pain. Her chest was hurting, her arms felt impossibly weak and empty, and every nerve ending in her body was strained to attention, listening for the sound of heavy tires crackling in the frost outside. She *needed* to see Bruce, and not only to see him — now that she knew how she felt about him, she needed very badly to know how he felt about her. That was, she realized, a very immature reaction. But just like the rest of it, there it was.

At midnight, she put the fire screen around the dark red, dying coals and went up to bed. The first night she had discovered she couldn't sleep in the bed they had shared and had gone back to the little room she had used at first. She went there now, forcing herself to shower and brush her teeth even though she felt exhausted.

He could have called, she thought angrily as she crawled in. *He could have let me know it would be another day.* But, she concluded bitterly, he probably hadn't give her a thought since he walked into his offices.

An hour later, the bedroom door crashed open and the light went on, startling her out of a deep sleep and half blinding her. Terrified, she jerked up, clutching the covers around her. Bruce stood in the doorway, staring at her.

"So, this is where you are. What in hell are you doing in here?"

He looked immense, filling the doorway, his dark face glowering. She burst into tears.

"*Damn* you, Bruce! I'm in love with you! I can't believe it . . . I've b-been so miserable, and I hate you for it . . . " Hunched in the small bed, she put her head down on her knees and wept.

Bruce had been worn out and disturbed when he left Atlanta. He had driven half the night just to get back to Elaine, and the empty house and barren big bedroom had frightened him. Typically, he had responded with anger. But now the anger was gone, as if it had never been, his face lined with fatigue, but the brown eyes were as soft as velvet.

"Make up your mind," he said gently. "Do you love me, or do you hate me?"

Elaine transferred her clenched arms from her knees to his shoulders, pushing her wet face into his neck. "Both! Never in my life did I want to feel like this . . . " She pulled away and looked at him with huge eyes like gray lakes, brimming over. "Do *you* love *me*?"

Behind the tenderness of the brown eyes, something stirred that looked suspiciously like laughter. "Very much. From the beginning."

"Good!" she snapped. "I hope you're miserable, too." But she kept on looking at him while his words sank down through her like a healing balm and her heart began to swell like an opening flower. The downturned corners of her mouth quivered and turned up. "Actually," she added shyly, "it feels wonderful, doesn't it?"

He didn't laugh, after all. "God, yes," he said huskily. "Yes, it does." Kissing her, holding her tightly, and then collapsing with her back onto the pillow, he buried his face in her fragrant hair and wished he had never gone to Atlanta. He had promised to free her of all her doubts, and all he had done was discover more problems. He sat up, pulling her up with him. "Come on, back to our bedroom. I need you. I'm afraid I'll go to sleep in the shower."

Elaine laughed, reaching for her robe. It was nice to be needed. "You won't even think about sleep," she told him, scrambling out of bed, "for at least an hour."

He didn't think about it then, either. When she grew drowsy in his arms, he insisted that she stay awake. "I don't want to sleep," he told her. "I want to make plans. When will you marry me?"

Elaine supposed it was logical, but she hadn't thought of it herself and she didn't want to start. How could she say she didn't like his life or his companions? She couldn't even look at him for fear he would see her thoughts in her eyes. She pulled her pillow over her face and lay there trying to think of some alternative to marriage. "I don't know," she said finally, her voice muffled by the pillow. "Someday."

"*Someday*?" He jerked the pillow away and stared down at her. "I'll give you a choice — next week, or the week after."

"Later." She looked at him hopefully. "Does that sound right?"

Bruce groaned and fell back on his pillow. "Later. How much later?"

Elaine moved over and put her head on his shoulder, yawning. "Well, you know — not right away." She was suddenly inspired. "We have so many other things to do, Bruce. There's the will to be probated, the estate to be settled, all those details."

Bruce stiffened slightly. "The will doesn't have to be probated."

Elaine raised her head. He looked perfectly serious. "Why not?"

He frowned. "Because a will is only

171

an instrument to distribute property and funds belonging to the person who made it. Frank signed everything over to you. House, car . . . "

"The car, too? Paul Somers told me about the house. He said he thought you'd checked earlier." She looked at him thoughtfully and added, "Beth Fenton tried to buy the car from me today, and she acted a bit surprised when I said I had to wait until the estate was settled. Do you think she knew?"

"I doubt it," Bruce said. "I'm sure Al didn't know. Frank must have done it on his own. Anyway, I also called the insurance company, and Frank had changed the beneficiary on that policy. It had been made out to his estate, but he gave them your name instead."

What had begun as curiosity had turned into the same old roil of pity and guilt. Elaine lay still, staring at the ceiling. "Well, there isn't much doubt, is there? He did his own distributing, because he knew he wouldn't be around. There's no other reason for giving everything away."

"One," Bruce said, and sat up. He

hadn't meant to go into all this in the wee hours of the morning when they were both so tired, but it had happened anyway. "What would you have done, Elaine, if Frank had come to you six months later and asked you to sign everything back to him?"

Elaine sighed. "I think you already know. I wouldn't have waited until he asked — I would have signed everything over to him again as soon as I found out he'd signed it over to me! I know it sounds ridiculous, but that's the way I feel. I wanted *nothing* from him. Since the day I walked out, I swore I'd never take another cent. He knew that."

"That's what I thought," Bruce said. "So he could have been planning to declare bankruptcy, invalidate his debts, and then quietly regain his property from you later. A very slick trick, indeed."

Elaine's eyes went wide. "But — Al would have known! He's his lawyer, and surely Frank would have told him."

"Hardly," Bruce said dryly, "since his major debt was the loan from Al."

She was silent, knowing Frank just might have done that. It would have been like him. He would have thought it both clever and amusing to pull it off, and maybe he had other plans that would work out to give him an income. So, maybe it had been an accident. She wanted so badly to think so.

"Then it's settled," she said finally. "I can just sell everything and pay off the debts."

Bruce looked down at her still-worried eyes and tense face and shook his head reluctantly. "Not quite, angel. There are a few more details."

"Like what?"

He lay down again and pulled her close, bringing up the covers and settling in. "Let's leave it for now. It's almost morning and details can be hard to explain. Just trust me, will you?"

Relaxing into his warmth, Elaine agreed sleepily. It was easy to agree; she always had trusted him.

8

AFTER Bruce finished his second cup of coffee after breakfast the next morning, he stood up and announced he was leaving. "A lot to do, angel," he added, kissing Elaine lightly, "but I'll definitely be back before dinner." In spite of yesterday's fatigue and a very small amount of sleep, he looked fresh and vital, the brown eyes full of life, his skin glowing with health.

"But, wait." Elaine protested. "You haven't told me anything. Is this to do with those final details you mentioned?"

He laughed. "Naturally. Since you won't talk marriage until everything is ironed out, you can be sure I'm concentrating on them. And, another thing, if we can all keep quiet about it, I'll set up the closing date with Somers." He turned to the door, and Elaine jumped up to follow him.

"Why do we have to keep quiet about it?" she asked, helping him into his bulky mackinaw. It had been a city lawyer who had come home last night, but a mountaineer was leaving this morning, complete in jeans and boots.

"I'd rather Fenton didn't know," Bruce said before he turned back to her. "If he finds out that we don't have to wait for probate, he might start bugging you for that loan."

"Oh." She was about to ask what difference it made, considering that Al knew he had to wait until the insurance money came, but she was suddenly enveloped in a cavern of loose mackinaw, crushed against a wide chest, and silenced by a kiss.

"Tell me again," Bruce said huskily, raising his head. "I need to hear it often so I'll believe it." He was still holding her, her arms were still around his neck, and she drew them away slowly, her hands caressing his bearded cheeks. She knew what he meant.

"I love you, Bruce McClure," she said softly. "Hurry back to me." Her eyes were full of silver promises.

He kissed her again, lingeringly, and felt his body react hotly. With a sound somewhere between a laugh and a groan, he let her go. "You're a potent little lady, ma'am. If I happen to be delayed somewhere, I may call and ask you to say that again." He left, his ears charmed by the soft ripple of laughter behind him.

On her way back to the kitchen, Elaine laughed again, this time at herself. She had intended to ask him all about details and what he hoped to accomplish, but she'd forgotten all about it with the first kiss. Or had that been the reason for the quick grab he'd made? Maybe he didn't want any questions right now.

In the next few days, she decided she'd been right. When she asked Bruce what he was doing in his frequent absences from the house, she was met by vague generalities and a change of subject. But they did go one evening to the office of the Eagle Real Estate Company and met with Paul Somers for the closing. And it was evident that Paul knew Bruce wanted it kept quiet. Paul remarked as they left that he'd wait a month before he recorded it.

"I'll open an account for you at the local bank," Bruce told her on the way back to the house, "and you can start paying that mountain of bills you've collected. I know they've been on your mind."

Elaine twisted in her seat, leaning back and facing him. They had been so happy together that it had almost obliterated everything else. But now she was intensely curious. "That isn't all that's been on my mind," she said. "I also keep wondering what's left to settle. It seems as if it should be simple now, but you're spending a lot of time on these details of yours, and you still haven't told me what they are."

Bruce's jaw tightened; she could see the line sharpen under the black beard. His eyes on the road, he seemed to be thinking how to answer her. When he did, she had the feeling he was choosing his words carefully.

"I made you a promise," he said, "and I'm trying to keep it. I don't want you going through life thinking you should have prevented Jeffrey's death." He looked across at her and smiled faintly. "It may be partly jealousy. I don't want you thinking of him at all."

"I don't think of him!" Elaine exploded. "Or if I do, it's only to think how glad I am that I escaped." She stopped, reaching to touch Bruce's arm. "I love *you*. I never loved him." She slid across the seat, needing comfort, and felt his arm go around her.

"I know you love me," Bruce said gruffly, "and I love you — too much to let this go on. You do think of Jeffrey, angel. Not with love, thank God, but with pity and guilt. I know you very well."

Elaine subsided, her head on his shoulder. He did know her, almost too well. There was no way to argue with the truth. But it seemed to her that if it was impossible to prove suicide, then it was also impossible to prove it had been an accident. She was sure he was wasting his time. Leaning against his warmth, she decided that no matter what he brought her in the way of evidence, facts or opinions, she was going to pretend to be completely convinced. Then he'd stop.

★ ★ ★

Elaine kept busy during the next week, sorting out the bills again, paying the oldest ones first, keeping a careful account. It took time, but she worked steadily until almost every penny of the money Bruce had paid for the house was gone. But the bills were gone, too; there wouldn't be a fresh flood arriving next month. She surfaced into a playful happiness that included no thought of the future. She teased her big bear of a man with imaginative lovemaking, cooked all of his favorite foods, and went with him on walks in the crisp weather.

Bruce loved it all, but he was also intent on what Elaine started thinking of as his mysterious business. He was in and out, gone for hours at a time, but she didn't question him. Then, the first of the next week, he left again for Atlanta and was away for another two days. Now that Elaine knew he loved her, it hardly made a dent in her happiness. But this time when he came home, he looked harried, the brown eyes lusterless, his firm mouth set grimly. When he looked no better after a good night's rest, Elaine began questioning.

"I'm just tired, love. There's nothing wrong with me." He smiled, pushing away his half-eaten breakfast. "Even if there was, I'd be cured by the sight of you this morning." His eyes ran over her caressingly, over the usual morning attire of skimpy jeans, the cream-colored velour top with its deep vee that barely contained the enticing roundness of her breasts. "You look good enough to eat."

"But breakfast didn't," Elaine said accusingly, coming to take away his plate. "I'm worried about you." She put the plate on the counter and came back to sit down opposite him. "Bruce, please listen to me. You're wearing yourself out with this — searching out clues or whatever and still trying to maintain your own business. It doesn't matter that much to me, really it doesn't. I want you happy and healthy. Please, darling, drop it."

The tired eyes slid away from her face. "I can't," he said abruptly. "I'm not in it alone. The insurance company is interested."

Elaine's eyes widened. She had wondered vaguely why there had been no word from the company, but she had supposed that it took time, maybe a lot of time when the payment was so large. "They're investigating? You mean they questioned the official report?"

His eyes came back to hers. "I told them," he said quietly. "I said there was a question as to whether the death was accidental or not. Naturally, they are looking into it thoroughly."

Elaine caught her breath. "I thought . . . " Her voice trailed away, her whole face changed, growing tight and pale. "You could have told me," she said bitterly. "You knew how I felt, how badly I wanted them to know. You must also know that I've been feeling like a rotten crook for not telling them myself! You and Al both treated me like an idealistic fool for even thinking of it!" She shoved her chair away from the table and leaped up. "I'm glad you went behind Al's back and told them anyway. But I'm furious that you didn't tell *me*! I guess trust goes only one way with you!"

"Hey!" Bruce reached for her, but she evaded his hand, heading for the door. "Elaine, wait . . . " He got to his feet and started after her, hearing her flying footsteps on the stairs and the distant slam of a door. Frowning, he went back to the kitchen, standing by the table as he finished his coffee. Then he went out to the foyer for his coat. He should have remembered, he reflected, how much total honesty meant to her. She probably really had felt like a crook, and hated it. But he just had a habit of keeping his decisions to himself — and there were some things he didn't want her to know. He'd give her time to cool off, and then explain as well as he could.

Pacing restlessly in the little bedroom upstairs, Elaine heard the front door close. Going to the window, she watched Bruce open the garage door, go in, then drive out. The big wheels ruffled sodden dead leaves as he went down the driveway, and she thought she felt as dreary as they looked. Another trip to town on business. With whom? The sheriff, sifting already sifted evidence? Or with the man from the insurance company? Maybe just with the men at the hunt club, who had been drifting away lately, going home for the holidays.

No matter what it was, he wasn't going to tell *her*.

She turned away from the window, no longer angry, merely empty and forlorn. Bruce was as evasive as Al Fenton ever tried to be, only better at it. He hadn't just fooled Al that evening, he had fooled her, too. It brought back the memory of most of the men she had known when she was with Frank. Sophisticated, knowledgeable men with smooth, smiling faces and some of the most devious minds she had ever encountered. Why hadn't she remembered that? She didn't belong in this crowd; she never had. She went on mulling it over until she caught herself wondering what Bruce's motive was in secretly telling the company her suspicions. He might save them a half million — was there an informant's reward? That thought was too much; she shook it off angrily. Bruce wouldn't do that.

She went downstairs to the empty rooms and began cleaning away the remains of breakfast. Looking around at the flaming colors, she wondered if now that Bruce owned the house he would have them changed. It was the first time she had really thought about the house belonging to Bruce now — not to Frank, not to her. She knew Bruce's plans; he'd discussed them a long time ago. He intended to make it his primary home. With Atlanta less than a day's drive away, a junior partner and an efficient staff in his office, he had said he could handle a great deal of business by telephone. He was looking forward to spending most of his time in his beloved mountains.

Elaine wandered back out into the huge living room and examined it as if for the first time. The ashes in the fireplace were dead; sun glinted through the wall of glass and struck splinters of light from the glass-fronted doors of the gun cabinet. Bruce had locked the cabinet and told her he intended to sell it, guns and all.

'It's nothing I want,' he had said casually. 'I have a couple of American-made guns, plain but accurate. They're enough for me. I hunt very little, and I'm not a collector.'

So, he could do that. He owned the

collection. That was on the contract — 'house and contents.' She turned away, going to the glass doors and looking down into the valley, wondering if she was part of the 'contents.' It was Bruce's house, and she was living in it. If they married, she'd go on living in it. The friends they would have would be his friends, her life would be his life. Admittedly, she didn't know any of the men at the hunt club except Al Fenton, but if they'd been friends of Frank's, she knew what they'd be like, and what their wives would be like, too. As far as she could see, the situation was the same as it had been before, with one notable exception. She had despised Frank, and she loved Bruce. She wondered painfully if she loved him enough, and if, with that kind of pressure, she'd go on loving him.

Behind her, there was a quick, sharp rattle of the knocker on the front door. Elaine turned, startled. Usually, she heard any car, but she'd been too immersed in her thoughts. Going quickly toward the foyer, she glanced through a window and saw the small blue and white Mercedes angled in carelessly against the line of shrubbery. Opening the door, she discovered Beth Fenton with her hand raised to knock again.

"Oh, there you are," Beth said brightly, lowering her hand. "I was afraid you hadn't heard me. Mind if I come in and visit a little?"

Elaine looked at her warily. "By all means," she said, rather proud of her choice of words, and stepped back. Beth was dressed casually today in heather slacks, and a hand-knitted harmonizing sweater, a long, loose leather coat, and a beret cocked saucily on her free-flowing blond hair. Slipping out of the coat, she hung it and the beret on the coat rack, looking around at the foyer, her bright smile fading to a solemn look. "Well," she said, "it brings back memories. Frank had me checking daily on the decorators." She gave Elaine a subtly challenging glance. "How do you like it?"

Elaine struggled to bite back a tart reply, then ended by nodding lifelessly and mumbling that it seemed appropriate and comfortable. She took Beth into the living room and busied herself in building a small but adequate fire.

"Could I offer you a cup of coffee?" Rising from the hearth, she forced herself to say it pleasantly.

Dropping into a chair, Beth fluffed her hair and gave a little laugh. "If you've brandy to put in it, yes. Coffee alone bores me." She glanced around the room as Elaine left and added approvingly, "I see you haven't changed anything."

Gritting her teeth in the privacy of the kitchen, Elaine made instant coffee and poured a generous dollop of brandy into one cup. In her present mood, she could think of nothing more depressing than having to deal with Beth Fenton and her prying tongue. With a sinking feeling, Elaine reminded herself that if she married Bruce and ran with the hunt-club crowd, she would be dealing with Beth Fenton on many occasions. Putting the cups on a small tray, she added the bottle of brandy and took the tray to the small table between the two chairs.

"There's brandy in your cup," she told Beth, managing a smile, "but I thought you might like more."

Beth nodded, sipped the coffee, and

promptly added more brandy. Sitting back with the cup in her hands, she glanced at Elaine coyly. "Where's your friend Bruce? I understand he spends a lot of time here these days."

"I see him frequently," Elaine said, her guard up. "After all, he's taking care of the estate. But I'm afraid I have no idea where he is when he isn't here." It was very easy to tell the truth.

Beth did her indecisive thing of opening her mouth and then closing it. Then, as usual, she jumped right in. "Well, I didn't make the trip up here to talk about your sex life, but I do think you need advice. Bruce McClure is using you, Elaine. He's dragging this out much longer than he needs to. Al says he's checked, and the will isn't even in the works for probate yet. And Bruce isn't doing it just to increase his fee, either. Like every other lawyer in Atlanta, he'd love to get in with Harrison and Toth. He's using Frank's longtime connection with them as an excuse."

Elaine barely managed to swallow an incredulous snort, and Beth smiled faintly.

"I can see you don't believe me, but I saw it for myself. I was over there Tuesday and dropped in on my father. There was Bruce, going over a bunch of old papers in my father's private office, talking away."

Elaine could think of absolutely nothing to say for a long minute. Then she smiled. "I see nothing wrong with that. Bruce is very thorough."

"But it wasn't necessary," Beth snapped. "Al is the partner there who handled Frank's business, and Bruce could have asked him anything he wanted to know. And, truthfully, there isn't anything to look into — he's just trying to ingratiate himself to my father. It's costing you more and it's irritating the hell out of Al. He's acting like a scalded cat." She sat up jerkily and poured brandy into her empty cup. "Not that I give a damn," she added morosely, "except that I have to live with him." She sat back again, sipping the brandy.

Elaine looked at the beautiful, discontented face curiously. Beth was a woman of contradictory tendencies, one time putting on a grand front, the next coming out with something amazingly honest. "I'm sorry your husband disapproves," she said diplomatically, "but I'd hesitate to tell Bruce how to handle a case. What did your father say was the problem?"

Beth laughed wryly. "My father is so ethical it hurts. If they'd been discussing the weather, he wouldn't have told me. Ask a priest in a confessional for the latest gossip and you'd get a fuller answer." She narrowed her eyes at Elaine and laughed again. "You're right, though. I did ask. I got a blank look and an invitation to lunch." She put her cup down empty and stood up. "Well, I've delivered the message, and I hope you'll take it to heart. Give McClure a little push, will you?"

Elaine rose and followed the tall, slim figure to the foyer. "I'll tell Bruce what you said," Elaine said as she held Beth's coat for her, "but I have no opinion to add. I trust his judgment." Saying it, she wondered if she still did.

"Don't," Beth said cynically. "All lawyers are tricky." Her greenish eyes were strained as she took another encompassing glance at the foyer, the graceful staircase going up, and then suddenly she burst into speech again. "Al finally got around to telling me that you were afraid Frank had killed himself," she said abruptly. "He said it worried you. Well, he didn't. It had to have been an accident."

Shocked, Elaine stared at her. "How do you know?" She had to ask; it was too important to ignore.

Beth was looking into the mirror, adjusting the tilt of her beret. "I *know*," she said flatly. "Leave it at that."

Elaine watched Beth stride swiftly out and get into the Mercedes, zooming away as if the devil were after her. Maybe it was her own lacerated feelings after the quarrel with Bruce that made her sensitive, but Elaine wasn't the least bit angry with Beth, only sorry for her. Under that bright, hard façade, there was a very unhappy woman.

Bruce came home late in the afternoon, noticing with a pang that no slender, pink-cheeked, smiling woman met him at the door. He tracked her down to the kitchen, where she had started dinner, feeling another pang as she turned and he saw the look in those huge silvery eyes. The anger was gone, replaced by a painful doubt.

"I'm sorry," he said gently. "I should have told you."

She put down the knife she'd been using, wiped her hands, and came to kiss him, the kiss sweet but tentative, her hands pressing against his chest as he pulled her closer. "It's all right," she said quietly. "I suppose I made too much of it. I'm very glad they know."

He was aching for a full, wholehearted embrace, a deep, I-love-you-kiss, but he let her go, knowing by the feel of her in his arms that she was still doubtful about him. "I am, too," he said, heading for the bottle of wine protruding from the clay cooler. "The investigator they sent is damned good. And quiet about it. No one knows he's here except for the sheriff and a few men at the club."

Back at the counter, Elaine looked dismayed. "The club? They'll tell Al."

Pouring wine, Bruce laughed. "No, they won't. Al isn't winning any popularity contests there. He never did." He picked up the two brimming glasses and brought her one, bending to kiss the curve of a delicate ear. "Can we talk about other things, angel? Like fine wines, and what it is that smells so good?"

She couldn't help the smile. She took the wine and sipped, looking at him. He was wearing a bright red flannel shirt with his jeans, and the color against the black beard and his white grin made him even more attractive, which he didn't need. If he were only a plain-spoken mountaineer instead of a slick city lawyer! Leaning against the counter, she drank deeply of the wine, feeling the pleasant warmth relax her tense muscles. There was no use trying to resist him. The small, cold place in her brain was vastly outnumbered by all the other cells in her body.

"A very fine wine," she said lightly, "and that's a casserole in the oven you're sniffing." She looked up at him, suddenly remembering Beth's visit, and added, "There is something more that we have to talk about, but it can wait until after dinner."

"Good." He moved closer, setting his glass down, taking her half-empty one and putting it on the counter. "Right now, I want my welcome-back kiss."

For a split-second, he thought he'd pushed her too fast, and then he felt her body yield, her mouth open under his with a little gasp, her arm tighten around his shoulders. His mouth grew fiercely possessive, his loins pinned her against the counter, moving, pressing into her softness. It was long, dizzying moments before he eased away, breathing hard, looking into her eyes to see the love he had to have. It was there, along with the soft warmth, the helpless desire. He relaxed, breathing easier.

"Don't go away from me again," he said gruffly, touching her cheek with one hand. "If we get mad, let's fight it out in bed."

Breathless, Elaine gave her little rippling laugh. "You'd always win."

"I'd probably never win," he murmured, holding her close again, "but it would be fun trying. Still mad at me?"

She shook her head, feeling the heat of silly tears, and moved away from him. "If this casserole burns, we'll both be mad . . . "

Dinner was pleasant. Bruce kept it

light, telling a series of anecdotes about courtroom blunders that kept Elaine laughing. A good many of the jokes were on Bruce himself as a young lawyer, and he told them with as much enjoyment as he told the others. In one corner of her mind, Elaine felt he was doing it mainly to distract her from the on going probe of Frank's death, but she didn't care. She decided she didn't want to know. She wasn't looking forward to telling him about Beth's visit, either, but once they had settled into their chairs near the fire, she knew she must. There was nothing about it of the slightest interest to her except for the certainty of Beth's final remarks, but there could be something of interest to Bruce.

Once she started, she recounted the visit word by word, not stopping to add her own thoughts, just repeating what Beth had said with as much accuracy as she could. Everything, including Beth's conclusion that Bruce was trying to cement relationships with Harrison and Toth. That brought an amused grunt from Bruce, but other than that he listened with total concentration.

"Then she said she *knew* it wasn't suicide," Elaine ended, "and left, as if she didn't want to say more. What do you think of it?"

"I think she was rough on you," Bruce said flatly. "I don't like that."

"I wasn't angry," Elaine said thoughtfully. "If anything, I was sorry for her. I don't think she would have come on her own, or said what she did. I think Al sent her." Telling the story, her own curiosity had been aroused. She wanted to ask what Bruce had accomplished by talking to Al's father-in-law, John Harrison. But she remembered what Beth had said about her father, and she was suddenly sure Bruce would be the same way.

"Of course Al sent her," Bruce agreed. "Beth has no interest in the case. And Al probably had more than one reason. He'd like to have the money for that note, for one. He would also like pointing out to you that he would have it all done by now. And well — I think he'd like to have it over and forgotten." Staring into the fire, Bruce looked as if he had something else to say, but then he sighed, stood up, and stretched, a mountain of man in the flickering light. Relaxing, he grinned at Elaine.

"If you're going to give me that push, make it in the general direction of the stairs. And come with me."

She went with him, knowing she always would as long as they were together. As long as she was still here, in this place with its aura of death, of secrets, its undercurrents of spite.

In bed, she went into Bruce's arms with a sigh of relief, knowing his lovemaking would drive away her thoughts and destroy her doubts. She wanted to drown the pain of their quarrel in a healing flood of love, taste the warm, dark glory of passion. And maybe Bruce felt the same; maybe he had something to forget, some pain that eased when he held her. Because it was one of those times when he took her to the edge of abandon again and again, then drew her back and started over, teasing, caressing, murmuring, and laughing, putting off that final losing of control that would take them to the heights and then bring them down once more to reality.

But finally it was there, a pleasure so

198

intense it shuddered through her like waves of fire, sweeping away tension and leaving her limp and utterly satisfied. It seemed wicked indeed to harbor the thought that floated through her mind . . . *Nothing lasts forever.*

9

EVEN in the grocery store, when her mind should have been on practical matters, Elaine thought of Bruce. He had become the yardstick by which she judged everything. The apples — had he said he liked them tart and crisp? The beef, since he might be tiring of game. Was that steak big enough? Buying wine, she bought only his favorites. It was silly, she knew. But she went on doing it, because she loved pleasing him and because, some realistic corner of her mind said, it might not last. She tried not to listen.

Driving home at noon, she saw the station wagon parked in front of the house. Her spirits rising, she parked and took the bag of groceries in one arm and dashed toward the door. Letting herself in, she heard a murmur of male voices and hesitated. Bruce, and a voice she didn't recognize. Entering the big room, she saw Bruce and a medium-sized man with a round, cherubic face turning away from the gun cabinet. The man was carrying a gun awkwardly, his wide, short-fingered hand wrapped around the barrel. Bruce smiled at her, but he looked awkward, too, and she was suddenly sorry she'd come in. He looked as if he was uncomfortable with her presence. Still, he came forward and introduced the other man as Rodney Townsend, and added that Townsend was the investigator for the insurance company.

"We're just taking care of some of those details," Bruce added vaguely.

Taking her cue from him, Elaine tried to ignore the gun, keeping her eyes on their faces, greeting Townsend pleasantly. Then she excused herself and went into the kitchen, glancing at the gun cabinet and seeing the empty niche that had held the dull, unpolished shotgun. So it *had* been the one that killed Frank. Otherwise, the investigator wouldn't have been interested in it. She swallowed, blindly putting away the food she'd bought. Then she heard the front door open and close and knew they were gone. The gun was gone, thank heaven. She shivered, depressed by the thought that it had been there ever since she moved in, subtly mocking. Frank's gun, in Frank's house. She wished suddenly and violently that Bruce hadn't bought this place. But he loved it; he would never want to live anywhere else.

Running up the stairs, she headed for the small bedroom, where she still kept her clothes. Changing into her usual jeans and soft top, she remembered the night in here when she had first told Bruce she was in love with him. They had been so happy. For that matter, the house had been the scene of all their lovemaking, but only when she and Bruce were together now did she feel at ease. In bed, in front of the fire, even in that crazy kitchen, when he was with her she could forget the way the house made her feel. But if they married . . . she sighed, thinking of the long hours she would be spending here alone.

Going back down the stairs, she thought of how it would be if she found an apartment and a job in Atlanta. It was scary to think about. She was used to small towns and very little competition, and braving a city with so little experience would be a big step. But it would be lovely to go on being lovers, to share the part of his life there and forget this place. There, when he was gone, she wouldn't just be waiting. She would have a full life of her own.

It began snowing, lightly but steadily, an hour or so before Bruce came home to dinner. Elaine watched through the wall of glass as the snow transformed the bare trees and frozen ground into a scene of beauty. It would soon be December, she thought, with Christmas only a short time away. And a new year, for new beginnings. If only Bruce would drop this impossible investigation and let Rod Townsend do it. It was Townsend's job, anyway.

When she heard the snow-muffled sound of heavy tires and the solid thump of the garage door going down, she rushed to open the front door for him. Bruce laughed and leaned down to kiss her, a firm, warm mouth between a cold nose and frosty beard. Then he struggled out of his mackinaw and took her in his arms for a deeper kiss.

"How sweet it is," he said softly, hugging her close, "to come home to a comfortable, warm house and a beautiful, very warm lady." Leaving one arm around her, he turned and started for the fireplace. Sniffing, he wheeled and changed direction toward the kitchen.

"Ah-h-h! How do you manage to create dishes with such heavenly odors, angel?"

Elaine laughed, looking at his vibrant grin, his eager dark eyes. Starving, as usual. "In this particular case," she said, "you start with venison. I made a ragout . . . " Her voice faded as she suddenly remembered whose hunting skill had filled that freezer. *Oh, Lord*, she thought frantically, *it's getting worse, not better*. None of these things had mattered at first, not until Bruce had bought the house and she faced the prospect of having to *stay* in it. She eased out of his arm as they entered the kitchen. "If you want to wash up," she said unevenly, "I can have dinner on the table in a matter of minutes."

For once oblivious of her feelings, Bruce lifted the top of the heavy pot and sniffed appreciatively. "Great!" His eyes swung to the clay cooler. "And Cabernet — even better. Be right back."

Elaine determinedly pushed the depressing thoughts away and began setting the table. Bruce was in a very good mood, almost exhilarated. Smiling, she put candles on the small table and took out the fanciest of the wineglasses to celebrate the occasion.

The hearty ragout, a crusty loaf of French bread, and a tarragon-flavored salad kept Bruce eating steadily. He surfaced only to give the cook extravagant compliments. Sated at last, he leaned back in his chair and smiled at her ruefully. "What a pig-out. My only excuse is no lunch, angel. And your kitchen magic."

Elaine smiled back at him. She loved to see him really enjoy the food she cooked. And the ragout had been even better than she had hoped. "I thought it was good, too," she said modestly. "I just don't have your capacity."

Watching her, his smile had turned from rueful to teasing. "Only one thing worries me — are you going to cook like that even after we're married?"

That wasn't fair. She hadn't expected that kind of attack, a teasing question that sounded so light, yet put her on the spot. She lowered her gaze defensively.

"I can't make a commitment to something that far in the future," she answered, keeping her own tone light. "I might forget how by then. Anyway, when I go back to work, I won't have time to spend hours in practice."

Bruce saw the defensiveness, the quick barrier that went up, heard the reference to her plan for going back to work. He hadn't lost his ability to catch the nuances of her emotions; he knew she was trying to slip away again. But he also knew now that she loved him, and he was counting on that. He brushed aside her attitude of reluctance. He *wanted* that commitment.

"It isn't that far in the future, angel. Rod Townsend discovered something today that may mean real progress. I think we'll wrap up all those details in one neat package before Christmas."

Elaine seized the chance to talk about something besides marriage. "Wonderful! I'd love to hear all about it, if you've gotten that far. Have you come to any conclusions?"

It was her turn, now, to see someone slip away. She watched the thick, stubby lashes shutter down over the brown eyes, saw the telltale ripple of muscle along the jaw beneath the black beard. He wasn't going to tell her a thing.

"There's nothing I can say, Elaine, I wish I could." His voice was very careful. "Remember, officially this is Townsend's inquiry, and I know he prefers to keep the details quiet. Anyway, no one can come to any real conclusions until it's over. With so many people involved, it could go either way."

It was such a typical answer from him. The same kind of answer she had been getting all along. As if the matter in question had nothing to do with her; as if she had no right to be concerned. She looked away, hurt and even a little angry. Without answering, she rose and began clearing the table.

Bruce sat there bitterly regretting saying anything about the investigation. He knew he should have anticipated her question. She was feeling left out and angry now, and he couldn't do a damned thing about it. It would upset her a hell of a lot more if he did tell her some of the things Townsend had unearthed. It was better to wait. He sighed and got up, moved close behind her as she worked at the counter, and put his arms around her waist.

"None of it has anything to do with the important part," he said gently. "What's important is *us*. The end of this probe, no matter what the decision, still has only one real meaning to me. It means that we can start doing some planning about the near future — not 'someday' or 'later'."

Elaine felt a quiver of fear, knowing what he was about to ask and not knowing how she could answer. If she kept putting him off without good reason, she could lose him . . . She felt his mouth touch her, moving sensuously along the sensitive skin of her neck, felt his arms tighten, one big hand smoothing upward to curl around her breast. She closed her eyes, feeling the delicious warmth of response, the sudden jolt of desire as his long fingers found the stiffening nipple.

That made her want to surrender and to give him anything he wanted. Pressing back against him, she turned her head, blindly seeking his mouth. If only he wouldn't ask . . .

Brushing her lips with his, Bruce looked at her closed eyes, the long black lashes lying against the ivory skin. He was still aware that she meant to evade the question of marriage. He thought he was beginning to understand why, and he knew he shouldn't force the issue. But she was trembling in his arms, wanting him, and he had to try. "New Year's," he said against her mouth. "We'll marry then. A new beginning, angel. A new life for us."

Her huge eyes opened and looked straight into his, frightened and stubborn. "I . . . listen, Bruce." Her lashes veiled her eyes again as she twisted around in his arms. Facing him, her hands sliding up to his shoulders, she bent her head and gazed at the middle button of his shirt. "I've been meaning to tell you," she said rapidly, "that I have a really good idea. I'm going to look for a new job in Atlanta. It will be perfect — with me living there, we can get to know each other very well, and — "

His hands left her back and fastened, hard, on her upper arms. "Elaine, *look* at me."

She felt helpless, held immobile by his strong hands, trapped between his big body and the counter. Both the helplessness and her desperation showed as she raised her face to his.

Bruce winced. "Angel, why are you so afraid?" Both wonder and pain were expressed by his deep voice. "Aren't you happy with me?"

Now, that was easy to answer. Her face cleared a little. "You know I am." Her hands slipped upward to circle his neck. "I've never been happier. I love you, very much."

He caught her to him roughly. "Then, dammit, marry me! You're driving me crazy. I think I know why you couldn't stand your first marriage — I've learned a lot about Jeffrey lately. But that's *over*." He hugged her, rocking a little, his face in her hair. He was pushing hard now for the decision he wanted, and he couldn't seem to stop. "Angel, you can't think it would be the same with me. I'm not Frank Jeffrey."

But she did think it would be the same with him, despite of their love for each other. Tight in his arms, she felt a leaden despair. Frank hadn't been able to keep her in this kind of life with his wealthy and immoral friends, and now she could almost hear his jeering laugh. The house he had left her was pulling her back into it. She could say yes, she could try living in this house — but how long would it be this time before she rebelled again?

"No, you aren't," she said, pulling away from Bruce. "You're nothing like him. But don't you see that everything *else* is the same? The same kind of life and the same kind of people around. You haven't really gotten into it yet, Bruce, but I have. I *know* what it's like." She turned away, unable to look at him. "It won't be just the Fentons — they'll be bringing his other friends, too. And how long would it be before you were the same? You — you're already evasive and deceptive with me, hiding things . . . " She whirled, her fear changing into a desperate anger. "You're better at that

211

than even Al Fenton! I can see through him, but *you* — you're like a wall! I have to stay here in this damned house and wait, never knowing *anything* — not where you are or what you're doing or whom you're with! I don't want that kind of life, and I don't want friends like that! I want to go on loving you, but I'm *not* going to marry you. I can't take the risk!"

He stared at her, speechless, trying to keep his temper down. He couldn't believe she had said those things, couldn't believe she had compared him with Fenton. Evasive? Deceptive? This *damned* house? Suddenly, a monumental rage, mixed with pain and intense disappointment, filled him and burst out of control. A red mist hovered before his eyes, obscuring the small, utterly defiant face staring at him. He whirled, this big man who was never awkward, and his violent movement sent dishes crashing from the counter into the sink, a wineglass shattering over them. He stared numbly at the broken glass and then grabbed it, crunching the pieces in his hand and flinging them into the trash can under the sink. His hand dripped blood as he braced himself on the counter, fighting to regain control. He needed badly to hit something, and there was nothing at all to hit. Suddenly, he lost the battle with himself. He turned back and faced the wavering image he could barely see.

"Then get out!" he roared. "Leave! If I'm so damned deceptive, what in hell would you want me for? Find your little job and crawl into your little shell and be safe! Go!" He waved a hand at the door and then looked at the hand, crimson with blood. Reaching behind him, he grabbed a towel, jerking it, tearing the holder loose from the wall. Wrapping the towel around his hand, he started for the door.

"Bruce!" Elaine barely got the word out of her nearly paralyzed throat, "I . . . " He had swung around at the door, and her voice failed at the sight of his face, Indian-red with tears of rage glittering in the brown eyes.

"Forget it!" he ground out. "You're a coward, Elaine! You said you were once, and you are. That's why you didn't want to fall in love with me, and why you *hated* me when you did! Now get out of my lousy, deceptive life!"

He strode on toward the front door, his heart pounding with his rage, and heard her running footsteps start behind him. Outside, he hesitated, his hand still on the nearly closed door, and shook his head, drawing in great drafts of cold air. The red mist before his eyes began to fade and he waited, listening. But the footsteps turned and went racing up the stairs. Bruce shut the door and went on, trying to make his mind a blank, trying not to remember what she had said, nor what he had said, either. He would think about it later, when his head cleared.

10

ELAINE had been dragging down suitcases from the top of the closet in the little room before Bruce had even managed to get the garage open and drive out. He had taken a look at his hand and had known it needed stitches. He drove on, glad for a reason to leave until he cooled down.

Elaine heard the heavy wheels crunch by below and knew it was for the last time. She went on packing, throwing her clothes into the suitcases, jamming them shut. She was numb with pain, thinking of nothing now except getting away before Bruce came back. It took only a half hour to gather everything up and get it all downstairs, piled around the front door. Throwing on her heavy jacket, she went out to get her car.

Thank heaven he'd left the garage door open. She brought the car to the front door and loaded it rapidly, got in, and then noticed her key to the house on her key ring hanging in the ignition. She worked it off, her fingers trembling, and ran back to lay it on a table in the foyer. This time when she came out, she turned and looked at the house. She knew dimly that leaving Bruce was going to hurt like hell when the numbness wore off, but leaving the house was like leaving a prison. *I* hate *it*, she thought with a sense of dull wonderment. Until this moment, she hadn't fully realized that. It loomed over her in the early evening darkness, and she saw it as just what it was — a monument to Frank Jeffrey's pride. His last extravagance.

Elaine stopped at the first motel at the next town. Driving with her hands trembling, her eyes full of tears, just wasn't practical. She didn't even care where she stayed, but she was at least lucky in her choice. The motel was clean and comfortable, the room far enough from the highway to be quiet. And the bed was good, even if she couldn't sleep for most of the night.

The flaring phosphorus lights outside sent a pervading gleam through a crack in the heavy draperies, and she lay staring at it as if it might illuminate her dreary thoughts. She had never seen Bruce so angry, but, then, she had never said such terrible things, such hurtful things, to him before. She had gone too far, and as usual she'd done it badly. He wouldn't forgive her — how could he? She couldn't forgive herself. He was nothing at all like Al Fenton, and right now she couldn't remember how she had managed to put him into a comparable class. Something about deception . . .

It could be for the best. At least it was a clean break, not as it would have been if she had married him and tried to live in that house and enter into that life while her love for him shriveled and died. She kept telling herself that until she almost accepted it. Then, grateful for the impersonality of the motel room, with no memories, no reminders, she finally dropped off into sleep.

She was still numb the next day, but at least she could drive safely. She arrived in the late afternoon, driving into the familiar small town of Scottsville with a sigh of relief. She had done some constructive thinking during the drive, realizing that she had left some unfinished business with Bruce. There was the car to sell, the insurance money to disburse once it came — if it did! If they reopened the case and decided Frank had killed himself, there would be no money to pay back to Al Fenton. Without Bruce to advise her, she'd just have to get another lawyer to deal with all of it.

Shrugging, she pulled into a parking space beside a neighborhood grocery near her apartment. That could wait until after Christmas and she knew what had happened. In the meantime, she needed something to eat.

The apartment was musty, and forlorn with the dead plants in their pots. Elaine opened windows to let the icy, fresh air in, turned on the refrigerator, and threw out the plants. Then, glancing at the clock, she went to the telephone and sat down, still in her heavy jacket. It wasn't quite five o'clock, and if she could catch her former boss, Lee Cramer, she might be able to pick up that reference tomorrow. Her bank balance was alarmingly slim.

"The reference?" Cramer questioned

warmly. "No, indeed, I won't give you one. I need you too badly myself. The secretary I hired found out yesterday that her husband is being transferred, and they're leaving tomorrow. You're a lifesaver, Elaine. Come back to work for me if you want the job."

"I want it," Elaine said, half laughing in relief. "I'll be there in the morning. And thank you!" She sagged back in the chair, letting her breath out, feeling better than she had since the argument with Bruce. Thank heaven she wouldn't have to go around filling out applications, being snubbed because she had so little experience. And she already knew the job, so there wouldn't be that tense, scary period there would be in a new position. One lucky break — maybe it was a sign that she'd done the right thing.

The air was fresher, so she closed the windows and turned up the heat. Unpacking her hastily packed and jumbled clothes, she thought again of that awful quarrel. Bruce had called her a coward and told her to go climb back into her shell and be safe. And that was exactly what she was doing — back in the same dead-end job, scared to try anything else.

What if I am? she thought, going to the bathroom to shower. *There's nothing wrong with being safe.*

★ ★ ★

It was a week later, when the shock had worn off and the numbness had disappeared, that she started seeing Bruce on the street. Men who really looked nothing like Bruce, but who turned their heads a certain way or wore black beards or were very large, yet walked lightly, with long strides. Sometimes it was just a deep laugh that made her turn around, then turn back and walk on, aching inside.

For a while, Elaine told herself that eventually it would wear off. It had to, because it wasn't possible to keep on feeling this miserable. She fastened her mind on her work. Cramer was beginning to expand his business of importing textiles and reselling them in the States, and there was a tremendous amount of correspondence, some of it written in English by foreigners whose quaint phrases at times made it as hard to translate as if they had written in their native language. She didn't mind; it kept her busy. But only during the day.

In Cramer's offices, none of the staff lacked opportunities for dating. There was a constant stream of men in and out every day. Importers, salesmen, buyers, and, twice, a man from an adjoining suite of offices who came in to ask Elaine out to dinner. He, she thought gloomily, was at least polite. Some of the buyers thought she went with the sale. But where she went was home, always alone, and what she discovered there was that it was, indeed, possible to keep right on feeling utterly miserable.

Morning after morning she assured herself that she would soon feel better, and evening after evening she found out she was wrong. Finally, there seemed to be only one solution. She had become convinced that Bruce had been right — she was a coward. Or she *had* been. She didn't have to *stay* a coward. Some things were more important than being safe.

The next morning she didn't bother to assure herself of anything. Instead, she gave notice.

Cramer looked pained. "If you need a raise . . . "

Elaine thanked him but refused. "The pay is right for this job, Mr. Cramer, and I like it here. But I want to go somewhere where there are more opportunities. Maybe — a city." She didn't say Atlanta; she wasn't sure she was quite that brave yet.

"But it's a poor time," Cramer protested. "If you give notice now, you'll be out looking during the week between Christmas and New Year's. Worst week in the year to find a new job. Why not wait until spring?"

New Year's. New beginnings. Elaine's heart leaped, sank, and leaped again. A yo-yo. "I won't mind," she said breathlessly. "I'll have to use some time in moving, anyway."

Christmas spent alone could be just another day in the year. Elaine came home one evening after working late and happened to glance up and see that her windows were the only dark blot on the apartment building. All the rest of the windows were blazing merrily with colored lights. She put hers up just to be cooperative, and then, inspired by their twinkling gaiety, she went shopping for herself, buying a Christmas-green hostess gown in softest velour, with a deep vee neckline. If, in the dim and misty future, Bruce happened to be around, he'd like the way it looked and the way it felt. And then, as a bonus, she bought an Atlanta newspaper.

Wearing the gown, she curled up in the only comfortable chair in the furnished apartment and studied the classifieds, both the Help Wanted and the Apartments for Rent. There seemed to be plenty of both. She was terrified at even the thought of going, cold, into a city and trying to make her own way, but she didn't intend to let the terror stop her. Even if she never saw Bruce McClure again, she was determined to learn how to be brave.

There were still three workdays left after Christmas, and they seemed to stretch before her like a month. She had made up her mind and shored up her courage, and she wanted to leave before she weakened. But the new secretary whom Cramer had hired to take her place was there to learn, and that made the time pass faster. On the second day, Elaine was at the files, explaining the system, when the telephone on her desk rang. The new secretary leaped to answer it.

"Mr. Cramer's secretary," she said importantly. Then: "Information about *whom*? Oh. No, I have no idea. . . but wait." She covered the phone with one hand and looked at Elaine. "Do you know anyone named Jeffrey?"

Elaine sighed, going to take the phone. "That's something else you should check out," she told the girl, "everyone's full name." She sat down. "Yes? This is Mrs. Jeffrey. How can I help you?"

"Let me count the ways," Bruce said unevenly. "There must be a million. How are you, Elaine?"

The coolly efficient secretary was now a quivering idiot who wasn't able to hold a telephone up with one hand. Elaine wrapped her other hand around the trembling wrist and managed to answer.

"Fine, thank you. How are you?" The words had never sounded so inane.

"Better now. Listen, do you realize you never even told me the name of the town you lived in? I've had missing-person bulletins sent to every coastal town in South Carolina and not one report back. Where are you?"

Confused, Elaine thought for a moment about that question. "*You* called *me*," she said finally, very carefully. "You must know where I am."

"Well, I don't! I happened to find a number you'd jotted down on the phone book, and the area code was right, so I took the chance. I thought it might be a friend, but I guess it's that bastard who fired you."

"He's not such a bastard," Elaine said weakly. "He hired me again."

"Thank God he did." Bruce was calming down. Elaine could hear him letting out his breath, a deep exhalation of relief. "You could have left me a note or something — some way to find you." The deep voice held a note of reproach.

Elaine was trembling, wondering if he could hear her heart pounding. "I didn't think you'd ever want to." She looked up, seeing the new secretary's fascinated gaze fixed on her face. She pointed at the door, and the young woman left, reddening.

"I deserved that remark," Bruce said, suddenly meek. "I said a lot of things to you that I didn't mean."

"And I deserved them," Elaine answered. "I must have been out of my mind. You aren't the least bit like Al Fenton."

Bruce laughed unsteadily. "I hope not. You aren't a coward, either. I've thought a lot about what you said, and I believe I know what you meant."

"I *was* a coward. You were right about that. But I'm not going to be anymore. Tomorrow is my last day on this job, and I'm going to find a better one. In — in a city."

There was a short silence in which she could hear him breathing. Then: "What city?" Now he was being careful, as if he thought she might disappear again.

Elaine eased back in her chair, feeling better by the minute. "I was thinking of Atlanta."

"You *were?*" Now he sounded hopeful, and then careful again as he added, "Were you thinking of looking me up?"

Her slender body felt warm again, after a long time of being cold. The corners of her mouth turned up. "It takes time to get over being a coward," she said, "but I think I might." The sudden thought of seeing him again, face to face was earth-shaking. "I'll be there next week. Want to give me your number?"

"I want you to come here first. Day after tomorrow."

Uh-oh. Elaine winced and closed her eyes. She had been afraid he might say something like that. Her new confidence fled.

"I guess I'm still a coward," she managed to say finally. "I can't, Bruce. Not because of you — I want to see you, very much. But . . . "

"I'll get you a motel room."

Her eyes flew open. Maybe he did understand. Or maybe he just didn't want her in his house. "Oh. Well, when I'm on my way to Atlanta, I could swing by there, I guess. But it won't be the day after tomorrow. I have packing to do. How about the day after?"

"No, that won't do. It has to be Thursday. The case is coming to a close, Elaine. Hanley has set up an informal meeting to have the new evidence presented. I think you should be there." He sounded very serious, very persuasive.

Oh, *no*. Elaine drew a deep, deep breath. Frank's death now seemed so far away, so unreal. She had pushed it to the back of her mind, and she didn't want it real again. And nothing could make it so real as to listen once more to that horrible description, the recounting of evidence. She could still feel the crawling guilt, the mounting nausea she had suffered at the inquest. She tried to speak, swallowed, and tried again.

"Couldn't you just tell me about it, afterward?"

"Elaine," he said gently, almost formally, "you owe me this."

Her heart sank and kept on sinking, drowning in dread. It was true, he had acted for her from the beginning. No matter how secretive he had been, and no matter what the verdict was going to be, she had to be there. She gripped the phone harder and cleared her throat.

"What time Thursday?"

"Four-thirty. And, since it will probably be a long session, you should be there early enough to have a good, substantial lunch. I'll make a reservation for you at Farley's."

She was silent, trying to plan. If she left late on Wednesday, stopped on the way, she could make it easily. "I can be there by three," she said, suddenly shaking again at the thought of meeting him. "At Farley's then."

"Fine. Oh, wait . . . "

Her hand had been wavering downward toward the phone cradle; she caught it back quickly. "Yes?"

"Do you mind if I ask you a personal question?"

"Why, no."

"Have you missed me?"

She made a small, confused sound and then came out with all her innate honesty. "Oh, Bruce . . . it's been *awful*!"

"Good!" The deep voice was unsteady

again. "I've been hoping you were miserable, too."

She hung up, wiping silly tears from her eyes. The memory of the night when she had loved and hated was sharp and clear.

11

THERE are times, Elaine decided, *when you can do the impossible.* By Wednesday night, everything that belonged to her had been removed from the apartment. She had packed as much as she could into the trunk of the little car and had boxed up lamps and mirrors, framed pictures, and knickknacks, and carried them off to a storage company, with the understanding that the boxes would be shipped to her when she gave the company her Atlanta address.

Tired but excited, she began the trip. During the hours before she stopped, she alternated between the wild hope that somehow in Atlanta everything would work between her and Bruce, and the frightened, depressing thought of that meeting with Sheriff Carl Hanley. She was too aware that the meeting could prove her fears justified. Some of the evidence must point to suicide, or there would be no reason to reopen the case. But maybe it would be a relief to *know*, no matter what they decided. Anyway, she had to go.

Thursday morning she was up early, ready to resume the trip. She liked to wear the most comfortable clothes possible while driving, so she put on old, soft jeans, one of the inevitable soft tops, with a warm jacket over it. She wove her hair into its thick braid and jammed a knitted cap down over it. She looked, she decided while putting on the cap, like a big-eyed immigrant, just landed. But she had made excellent time and she knew she'd arrive at Farley's by two-thirty. She intended to use the half hour before Bruce arrived to change into something suitable and attractive.

Driving in the foothills of the Appalachians was slower by far than following the coastal highways; nevertheless it was just two-thirty when she pulled in at the immense Farley motel complex. Registering at the desk in the impressive lobby, she offered the clerk her MasterCard.

"It's all taken care of, ma'am," the

clerk said, pushing the card back and handing her a map of the complex, "on an open ticket." She smiled winningly. "That means you can just sign your slips in the lounge and the restaurant. Now, here is your room on the map, and this is your parking space. Drive west past the recreation area and turn south."

Map in hand, Elaine went back out to her car. It had been very generous of Bruce, but she could have afforded a room, even at Farley's. It was a little embarrassing. She kept wondering about that clerk's smile.

Driving around to the west, she found the place glaringly empty. Only a handful of cars was dotted among the parking spaces, a tenth of the number she had seen here in the early hunting season. Then, turning south, she looked along the long line of empty spaces, and her heart leaped up and lodged in her throat. There was no mistaking the battered wagon parked near where she was headed, and she knew the silhouette of the big, bearded man inside very, very well. Parked there and waiting at two-thirty?

She slowed, her hands shaking nervously, the car weaving a little. She looked terrible! her thoughts circled wildly. Whip around and go back to the lobby? Maybe she could find a restroom and change, or at least comb her hair . . . She groaned, looking ahead again. He had recognized her car and was getting out, *and* beneath his mackinaw he was wearing that red-and-black-plaid shirt! That was *cruel*. With a whimper of despair, she drove on, bumping into a parking space awkwardly and stumbling over her own feet as she got out.

"You're too early," she accused, looking up at him. She had forgotten, after all, how big he was. And how magnetic. He looked *wonderful*, and her whole body quivered, demanding to be flung into his arms. "I was going to . . . to change into something decent . . . "

Bruce reached for her, crushing her full length against him, stopping her flow of words by simply pressing her face into the curve of his shoulder. Her arms, those surprisingly strong, slim arms, found their way unerringly under his open mackinaw and around the taut, muscled torso. Without any instruction from her they fastened themselves tightly and clung. She breathed in his scent of warm skin and wool, of something else that was peculiarly him and absolutely necessary to her health and well-being.

"Sh-h-h!" he was murmuring. "Just let me hold you a minute. Anyway, you look beautiful." His hand moved over her head and closed on the braid hanging below her cap, tilting her head back so he could look into those big, expressive eyes. And what he wanted was still there. Something lovely, something tender, something he knew now he couldn't do without. The constant leaden fear he had felt ever since he discovered she had gone suddenly disappeared, leaving him feeling light as air and ridiculously happy.

"I love you, too," he said, illogically, since she hadn't said a word, and then he kissed her. A welcome-back kiss that lasted until the sound of a car stopping and the slam of a door alerted them to the fact that they weren't alone. They broke apart hastily, and without a word moved to the trunk of her car. Opening the trunk, Bruce stared.

"All this? Good Lord."

Elaine laughed tremulously. "Only the two bags on top. The rest of it can wait until I find a place in Atlanta. You've forgotten — I'm moving."

"I hadn't forgotten. Who's thinking?" He lifted the two bags out and shut the trunk, staring down at her with bemused eyes. "Where do you want these?"

She stared back at him. "My room?"

He looked a moment longer and then broke into laughter. "That sounds right," he said, tucked one bag under an arm, took the other in the same hand, wrapped the other arm around her, and headed along the line of doors. "I'd better start thinking. We haven't much time if we're going to have a good meal before that meeting."

Trying to match his stride, Elaine felt her dread of that meeting trying and failing to break through the solid, protective wall of happiness. Watching as Bruce unlocked and opened the door of the room, she knew she could stand anything as long as he loved her. She went in, glancing at the luxurious room with its king-size bed and extravagant appointments. There was a separate dressing room, thank heaven. She grabbed the right bag out of Bruce's grasp and headed that way. "I'll hurry," she said over her shoulder. "I know your appetite."

He grinned and dropped into a chair, reassured by the sparkle in her eyes, the flushed cheeks, that enchanting smile. He knew his appetites, too. Right now his body was putting up a vigorous argument for joining her in the shower, while his mind was telling him to be cautious, to wait. It was possible that after this evening she might need a lot of comforting, and comforting could lead very naturally to making love. He was a little ashamed of the thought — very little. He needed comforting, too.

Elaine came out dressed in a plain navy-blue suit, strictly tailored. In the high-collared Victorian silk blouse, and with her hair knotted sleekly above her slim neck, she looked prim, virginal, and somehow intensely desirable. The movement of her rounded hips was subtle and smooth in the fitted skirt; Bruce's hands remembered precisely the feel of her breasts under that silk blouse. He sighed and got up quickly, grabbing her coat and heading toward the door. He had to get her out of this room and away from the sight of that inviting expanse of bed.

"We'll eat at the restaurant here," he said, ushering her out. "It's convenient, and the food is good."

They managed to relax over a meal that was more like a dinner than a lunch. Bruce asked her about the work she had been doing in Scotsville and what she wanted to do in Atlanta, and ended up by saying that if she was really determined to go there, she could use his apartment until she was settled. "It would make things simpler," he added.

Elaine looked him in the eye. "I'm sure it would," she said in a tone that implied she wasn't the only one who would find it simpler. "But I'm also sure I won't have any trouble finding a place of my own." At his crestfallen look, her mouth curved into a teasing smile. "I'll love visiting, though, when you're in the city."

Bruce grinned and was silent. He had plans of his own.

At a little after four, they drove down into town and parked on the dusty street where the sheriff's offices were located. A medium-size brick building and a parking lot with two cruisers housed the entire law-enforcement body serving the small county. They left the car, joining a group of men already standing in front of the building. Strangers to Elaine, they all nodded pleasantly to Bruce, and two of them came over to shake his hand.

"Hope it goes the way you want it, McClure," one of them said. The other grinned and added, "Good luck. You may need it."

"Always," Bruce said, smiling, and introduced them to Elaine. Shaking their hands, she looked at them curiously. Natives, she thought. Big, bluff men with an air of the outdoors about them, but they didn't really look like the local farmers. They appeared to take on an expression of wariness when they heard her name.

"That was rough about Jeffrey," one of them said uncomfortably. "Not the kind of accident you'd expect him to have."

Another man had joined them in time

to hear the remark. "Hell," he growled, "I sure don't miss him. I hope Fenton leaves, too. We can do without men like them."

The first two men were stiff with embarrassment. "Dick," one of them said, sounding strangled, "this is Mrs. Jeffrey."

The man named Dick turned beet red. "I apologize ma'am. I wouldn't have said that for the world, if I'd known. I've got a big mouth."

"It's all right," Elaine said quickly. "I say what I think, too. And I'm often in trouble over it."

Bruce laughed. "I don't think I can add anything to that," he said, turning Elaine toward the building, "not safely, at least. I see we can go in now. Someone is unlocking the door."

Going past the small front office and a desk where a deputy sat, they entered a larger room in the back of the building. There were several men there when they arrived, milling around, putting papers down on a large table, setting chairs along the walls. Elaine recognized the sheriff, Carl Hanley, and also Rod Townsend the

240

insurance-company investigator. There were two uniformed deputies, a clerk, and another man, who caught her eye because of his clothes. The expensive, three-piece suit was unusual in this gathering; his sleek hair was cut fashionably. He was already seated at the table, frowning over a sheaf of papers.

Bruce seated her at a chair along the right wall, conferred briefly with the sheriff, then came back to sit with Elaine.

"Who were those men outside?" she whispered. "Natives?"

Bruce shook his head. "Members of the hunt club. They aren't witnesses, but they're interested. I think Carl will let them stay."

Elaine sat back, puzzled. They certainly hadn't looked like Frank's usual crowd. Or sounded friendly to him, either. Maybe Frank and Al had bought into a place where they weren't wanted. Maybe she had been wrong about a lot of things. She looked up and forgot about it as Beth Fenton came in.

Beth looked haggard and strained in spite of a handsome dark green suit and a fur coat that she tossed carelessly on the back of her chair. With her was a tall, distinguished-looking man with gray hair. He sat down beside Beth, his lined but good-looking face dignified and impassive as he swept the room with a glance. Seeing Bruce, he nodded in recognition. Bruce acknowledged the nod with a slight smile, leaning down a minute later to Elaine's ear.

"John Harrison, Beth's father. I'm glad he came."

Elaine wanted to ask him why, but her attention was drawn to the table. Sheriff Hanley had taken a place beside the well-dressed man; Rod Townsend sat on the sheriff's other side. Hanley's eyes traveled the room, checked the clerk beside the table with her pad and pencil, glanced over his shoulder at the deputy standing behind him. Satisfied, he began to talk.

"I think you all know that new evidence has been brought in about Frank Jeffrey's death. We're here to consider it." He glanced at the men in the back of the room. "This isn't a public meeting, but if there's no disturbance the spectators can stay. Now, we've called one new witness, and after she has her say, we'll review the written depositions of the witnesses at the inquest. After that, we'll get around to the new evidence." He looked at a short, matronly woman on the opposite side of the room. "Hester, come over here and take the chair in front of the table, if you don't mind."

The woman rose and awkwardly made her way to the chair, and while she settled herself Hanley addressed the room again.

"This is Hester Furman, wife of Henry Furman, who owns the farm where the accident occurred."

Interested in spite of herself, Elaine detected a glint of amusement in the the eyes of the well-dressed stranger at the table. Well, maybe the sheriff's informality did verge on comedy, she thought, but Carl Hanley had a real dignity of his own. And he made things plain.

"Hester," Hanley continued, "we want to hear what you remember about Mr. Jeffrey and Mr. Fenton coming to the farm that day."

The woman was clearly ruffled. "Like

I told you, Carl, there's nothing to tell. I saw them from my kitchen window when they drove up, and I went out. Mr. Jeffrey was laughing, I guess at something Mr. Fenton had said, and then he jumped out of the Jeep and came to ask me where Henry was. I told him Henry was out cutting wood. Then he asked me if I knew where it was that Henry had seen that big buck. I told him on the edge of the north pasture, down by the branch. He was grinning all over his face, telling me he was going to get that buck. Then he jumped back in the Jeep and they drove off."

"So he was in good spirits?"

She nodded. "Just like a kid. Like he always was."

"All right, Hester. Thank you."

The woman went back to her chair, and Hanley looked around at his deputy. "Get Tom for me."

Disappearing through a door, the deputy came back with another uniformed man, who took the empty chair. Hanley picked up a typewritten sheet and in a droning voice read Thomas Brown's report of the scene at the farm.

Elaine shut her mind away as the droning voice described the sagging fence, the position of the body, the angle of the tangled gun, and the extent of the wound. Brown also had described the gun, a Fortner double-barrelled shotgun, one barrel discharged, the other still loaded with buckshot. Brown said he'd unloaded the remaining shell and brought gun and shell with him back to the sheriff's office. Hanley put down the paper and looked at the deputy.

"Where's the gun now?"

"Mr. Fenton came and got it after the funeral and took it back to Jeffrey's house. It's a fine gun, and I guess he didn't want it to get lost."

"Any changes you want to make in this deposition, Tom?"

"No, sir. That's what I saw and that's what I did."

Hanley pushed the paper toward him. "Sign it again, then, and date it today. Then bring me Forbes."

As the deputy left, Hanley looked up. "For those of you who don't know, Len Forbes is our medical examiner."

Forbes, a lean, enigmatic-looking man,

came in and sat down silently. Hanley, scanning a new sheet, laid it down.

"Len, this jargon is pretty technical. Suppose you just tell these people about it."

Forbes began talking as if he had anticipated the request. "Our measurements indicated that the distance between the gun barrel and the body coincided with the spread pattern of the buckshot. The angle of the entering shot was correct, and the nature of the wound indicated that Fenton's decision of instantaneous death was accurate. There was no alcohol or other drugs in the blood. In other words, every test showed that the death occurred exactly as Mr. Fenton testified."

"Thank you, Len. Please sign again and date it." Hanley leaned back in his chair and spoke to the deputy. "Furman, please."

Elaine wondered at the tension in the room. This was all just a simple recounting of the things they already knew, yet everyone was silent, staring and listening intently. There must have been rumors, but, then, in a small town, there were always rumors. Watching Furman come in, she thought she would have known he was a farmer. He had the weatherbeaten skin and knotted muscles, the slight stoop to the shoulders. He was wiping his face with a handkerchief as he sat down to listen as Hanley read his report.

Furman had said he'd been cutting wood in a stand of trees on the hill that overlooked the field. He had heard the shot and decided to look since he had two cows in that pasture. He had reported seeing Mr. Fenton bending over Mr. Jeffrey, who was tangled in the fence, and he'd guessed right away what had happened. Then, he said, Mr. Fenton had stopped trying to get Mr. Jeffrey out of the fence and had stepped away, looking shocked. When Fenton grabbed up his own gun and ran for the jeep, Furman said he'd feared the worst. He had gone down to see for himself, and it had made him all shaky. He started to take the gun away, but then thought the sheriff would want him to leave it. So he'd gone back up to the woods. No disrespect to the body intended, he'd added; he just couldn't stay there.

"Now, Henry," Sheriff Hanley said, laying down the paper, "you remember when you made this deposition, I asked you why you wanted to remove the gun and you told me it looked evil, like it might do more damage. Seeing how shook up you were, I can understand your feelings. But I want to know if you moved the gun in any way."

"Nope," Henry said, mopping his face again. "I gripped the stock and tried to loosen it, but it was firm in the tangle. She didn't move."

"Thank you. Now, one more question. How far did you have to walk from where you were cutting wood to the edge where you could look down into the field?"

"I didn't have to walk, Carl. Just stand up and turn around. I was right there at the edge, picking up deadfalls."

The sheriff nodded and handed the papers to the clerk. "Get those questions and answers typed up on there and bring it back for Henry to sign, Mary."

The clerk took the paper and left the room. In the silence that followed, Elaine could hear Bruce's steady breathing, the sounds of the men in the back of the room as they shifted their weight and whispered to each other. Across from her, John Harrison and his daughter Beth were like wax figures, his face still impassive, her face an autocratic mask. At the table, the strange man no longer looked amused, just thoughtful. The sheriff looked the same as always, and Rod Townsend's round, cherubic face was blank. Elaine dared an upward, sideways glance at Bruce and found his deep brown eyes looking at her with an expression that jolted her to her toes. Hastily, she whispered the first question that came into her mind.

"I forget — are there more witnesses?

Bruce's faint smile showed he knew his look had shaken her and he didn't mind at all. "Only Fenton, I think."

Slightly ruffled but not displeased, Elaine settled herself to listen again as Fenton came in. He came lightly, confidently, looking a little impatient. He smiled at his wife and father-in-law and sat down in the chair in front of the table. Catching sight of Elaine, he raised his brows and smiled again.

Sheriff Hanley cleared his throat. "What I'm going to do, Mr. Fenton, is read your deposition to you. Like the others, if you hear something wrong, you can mention it. At the time, you remember, we considered we all knew what happened, and maybe some of us were careless."

"Sure, Carl. I know you have to do this." Al's gaze swept Rod Townsend insolently, placing the blame.

Hanley began reading. Al had described the whole day, from the time Jeffrey came to his house, left his car, and got into the jeep. They had hunted, he said, all morning without finding game. So in the afternoon they'd gone to Furman's farm. They had stopped at the farmhouse and Jeffrey had talked to Mrs. Furman. Then they had ridden around on the farm road to the north pasture. Parking on the road, they had separated to approach the field, cross it, and enter the woods. Fenton said he was just at the fence and preparing to ease through when he heard a shot. He looked up and saw Frank tangled in the wire about a hundred yards away, and he took off running to see if Frank was injured. He dropped his gun to help Frank out of the fence, but when he leaned over him he knew he was dead. It had shaken him badly. He had grabbed up his gun and had run toward the Jeep with some crazy idea of getting a doctor, but by the time he got to the farmhouse he'd known he'd better call the sheriff. He'd waited there to lead the deputy to the scene.

Laying down the paper, Hanley looked at Al. "Any changes, Mr. Fenton?"

Al shook his head. "No. It's correct." He sat up and took out a handkerchief, wiping his eyes and blowing his nose. "It brings it all back, Carl." He stood up. "Want me to sign it?"

The sheriff sighed. "No, Mr. Fenton, I don't. I have questions. You remember at the other inquest that Henry Furman testified that while you were gone he went down and looked at Mr. Jeffrey's body."

"Yes, I do remember. As I recall, he was cutting wood up there and came to investigate because he heard the shot."

"That's true," Hanley said. "But in further testimony today we discovered that Furman was on the edge of the woods at the time. He heard the shot, stood up, and turned around and saw you bending over Jeffrey's body. And I just don't think you could run a hundred yards in the time it took Henry to stand up and turn around."

There was a deadly silence in the room. Al still stood, staring at the sheriff, his long face turning pale.

"What are you trying to do to me, Carl?" he asked quietly. "Rig the evidence? Why let Furman change his story?"

"He didn't change it," Hanley said dourly. "I have to admit it was our mistake. We just took it for granted he'd had to walk a spell through the woods. This time, I asked him."

"I see." Al sat down again, passing one hand over his face, slumping for a moment against the back of the chair. Then, taking a deep breath, he straightened. "All right," he said dully, "I was closer. A lot closer — no more than six feet away. I guess I lied about it to keep from having to tell what I saw." He turned his head slowly and looked at

Elaine, then back at Carl. "His wife was right, Hanley. Frank killed himself."

A shock wave ran through the room. There were audible gasps, a deep rumble of sound from the men in the rear. Elaine was struck by a sense of true tragedy; a dizzying nausea churned in her stomach, a gray mist wavered before her eyes. Then Bruce's hand, warm and strong, gripped hers. She shut her eyes against the mist and held on.

"I guess you'll have to explain that," Hanley said calmly. "We'd like to have the truth this time, Fenton."

"You'll get it," Al said bitterly, "and I'm betraying a friend." He was rigidly tense, his pale eyes impenetrable. "I know that new evidence you have includes the note Frank sent his wife a few days before he died. Well, the note meant just what she thought it meant. Frank Jeffrey was broke, and he couldn't live that way. He began talking of taking the easy way out, telling me his insurance would pay all his debts and leave his wife well off. He kept saying it would be easy enough to 'arrange' an accident."

Every word was like a physical blow

to Elaine, but with Bruce's hand holding hers she was determined to be brave. Or if not brave, to act like it. She opened her eyes, seeing that across the room Beth Fenton was leaning forward, her greenish eyes blazing, staring at Al.

"I argued with him of course," Al was saying. "I did my level best to talk him out of it. And I thought I had when he quit talking about it. But out there in the field . . . " He stopped, swallowing. "It was quick. He had started through the fence ahead of me and I saw him stop halfway, between the wires. I thought his clothes had caught on the barbs, and I started over to help him. When . . . my God, I saw him hugging that gun and easing his other hand down to the trigger. I jumped to stop him, and the gun went off . . . " He put a hand over his eyes and sat there, trembling.

"He's lying." Beth Fenton was on her feet, her face livid with shock and hatred. "I suspected him before, but he swore it was an accident. He — he *killed* Frank." Her voice rose, out of control. "*Didn't* you, Al? You killed the man I loved because you knew I was leaving you!

254

Damn you to hell!"

John Harrison was on his feet, his arms around Beth, urging her back down into her chair. Al had twisted to look at her, and now he turned back, desperately trying to stay calm as he faced Hanley again.

"She's right about one thing," he said raggedly. "I knew they were lovers. But I didn't hold that against Frank. He sure wasn't the first one."

"You bastard!" Beth shouted. "You cold bastard! What you hated losing was my money!" She struggled against her father's arms and then collapsed against him, crying noisily.

Carl Hanley shuffled papers on the table, embarrassed. "Mr. Harrison," he said, "if you'd like to take your daughter out, it's all right with me."

Harrison, his hair disheveled from the struggle, his eyes agonized, nodded and stood up, pulling Beth with him. His arm around her, he took her out, shutting the door quietly behind them.

To Elaine, the scene had taken on an air of complete unreality. It all seemed like a movie, including Al's description of Frank killing himself. It had been so dramatic, and Al did it so well — like an accomplished actor. She shook her head to clear it and glanced up at Bruce. His face was grim, the brown eyes worried as they scanned her. She tightened her slim fingers around his hand.

"I don't believe him," she whispered, and saw the worry leave his eyes.

"Good for you, angel," he said softly. "I was afraid you would."

They drew apart as Hanley spoke again. "Naturally, Mr. Fenton, your wife's remarks will not be recorded as testimony. And you're right, we do have the note you spoke of, and what Jeffrey wrote could be taken that way. But we have other evidence that points in another direction. Three days before his death, Jeffrey filed two legal actions: one for bankruptcy, the other a divorce action against Elaine Colton Jeffrey on charges of desertion. If a man was going to kill himself, those two problems would solve themselves, wouldn't they?"

Elaine gasped, her cheeks coloring as faces turned toward her. Bruce leaned forward, a massive shield between her and the curious eyes. Still flushed, Elaine kept looking past him at Al.

"That's hard to believe," Al was saying harshly. "I handled all Frank's legal affairs. He wouldn't have gone to another lawyer."

Hanley shrugged. "We have photostats, if you care to examine them."

"I'm not interested," Al snapped. "I've told you all I know, Hanley. Maybe Frank did waver between one course and another — a man has to be close to insanity at a time like that. But in the end, he chose to take his own life. I *saw* him do it, remember!"

Hanley sat forward, his heavy face set in grim lines. "So you said, Fenton. But that's not all the evidence. You may want to make another statement when you hear the rest of it."

"No! Townsend is satisfied, and you ought to be!" Al's voice was high-pitched, snarling. "You'll get a kickback from the insurance company, won't you? You just saved them a half million, Carl! They're bound to be grateful."

Hanley glared at Al, his grim face going dark red. "That's more than enough, sir!"

He swung to look at the well-dressed man on his right. "Well?"

The man nodded abruptly and Hanley turned to his deputy. "Read Mr. Fenton his rights," he ground out. "I'm arresting him on suspicion of murder."

The noise was deafening. Al was shouting, the men in the back of the room were milling around and talking loudly, and Hester Furman uttered a thin scream. The sheriff was calling for quiet and then yelling to clear the room.

"Let's get out of here," Bruce said, pulling a stunned Elaine to her feet. "It's over. Dammit! I wanted the rest of the evidence presented." Holding Elaine protectively, he pushed through the crowd of men. One of them reached over and clapped Bruce on the back.

"Way to go, Bruce! When I saw the state's attorney nod at Carl, I knew you'd done it. Nice work."

"Tell Townsend that," Bruce said, and pushed on.

12

OUTSIDE, Bruce drew Elaine aside from the door to allow space for the excited, noisy groups coming out behind them. "If you don't mind," he said, "I'd like to wait for Townsend to come out. I want to speak to him."

Elaine nodded numbly. She didn't mind at all; she needed a moment to stand still and take it all in. In the early darkness, the dusty little street was transformed, all the harsh outlines softened, all the buildings twinkling with many-colored holiday lights. Snow was falling lazily, just a dust of silver-white on Bruce's black hair.

She shivered, buttoning her coat and breathing deeply of the fresh air. She felt completely exhausted, emotionally drained, yet she was full of a peace she hadn't felt since that note had fallen out of its envelope. It *wasn't* her fault that Frank had died. In fact, she thought, it was Frank's fault. He had finally run up against a husband who refused to be cuckolded — that was, if this were all really true.

Townsend came out, and Elaine watched Bruce step over to meet him. They stood there, talking in low tones, and she went on with her thoughts. All this time, she had thought that note was a hidden plea for help, that Frank needed her. And he'd written it the same day he'd filed for divorce! It was almost funny. That divorce was what he had alluded to when he said she'd be free at last. But only now was she truly free. And it felt wonderful.

She looked up and smiled as Bruce came back to her and took her arm. "You're going to have to explain it to me," she said as he piloted her along the dark street, "but I want to tell you I'm glad I came. I needed to hear that."

"You would have heard it all if Al had been willing to listen," Bruce said. He looked exhausted, too, the lines in his cheeks deeper. "I was sorry I'd made you come when he switched to that note and the suicide angle. I should have known he would when things got tight. He did it damned well, I thought."

"Too well," Elaine said. "Like a well-rehearsed actor. He really did kill Frank, didn't he?"

"Yes." They had reached the wagon, and Bruce opened the door for her. Going around, he climbed in and started the engine, letting it warm up. He glanced at her small face, seeing the blue smudges of fatigue around the silver eyes. "Are you sure you want to hear about it?"

"Yes, I do," Elaine said firmly. "Tonight — and then never again."

Bruce smiled. "That's a bargain, angel. We'll clear it up and then forget it. To begin, when I first suspected that Al had killed him, I — "

"Wait," she interrupted. "When and why did you suspect Al?"

Bruce laughed a little. "I almost hate to tell you. I'm supposed to deal in fact, not fancy. But I suspected him from that night we met at . . . well, it was your house at the time. I've seen Al in court, and he's usually cool and collected under any circumstances. You saw that, tonight. But that night, when you sprang on him about Frank's death not being an accident and mentioned that you had proof, he lost control completely. He was *scared*. He jumped to the conclusion that you meant murder and he acted like a fool. Ordinarily, Al's the kind who would have raised his eyebrows and asked you to clarify your statement."

"I see," Elaine said, "but I certainly didn't at the time. He practically accused *me*."

"Smokescreen," Bruce said, backing out of the parking space and starting slowly along the brightly lit street. "Anyway, I knew if what I thought was true, I had to find a motive. I started with John Harrison, and after he learned the situation he was open with me. Frank had filed the bankruptcy and divorce actions through Harrison to keep Al from finding out, and Harrison also knew that his daughter was planning to divorce Al and marry Frank. He deeply disapproved, but Beth is his one weakness. He can't deny her anything. So, I had my motive, but I wasn't sure Al even knew it. And I certainly didn't know how Al could have managed to murder Frank in such a situation. That's when I called the people at the insurance company and asked for their help, which of course they were willing to give. They sent Townsend, who is a fine professional detective."

Elaine had gotten caught up in the story as if it were a puzzle, not reality. "Why would it have been hard for Al? Couldn't he kill Frank first and then put him in the fence?"

"You heard Len Forbes," Bruce said. "Every measurement had to be exact. The gun had to be at the right angle, the right distance. And, while they didn't mention it, the blood from the wound had to be in the right spot. They would have checked it all, and if there had been any discrepancy, Al would have been on the carpet long ago."

"Then I don't see how he did it, either," Elaine said slowly. "Frank was athletic. He would have put up a struggle."

"He never had a chance," Bruce told her. "Townsend reconstructed it for me, and I'm sure he was right. Al had an identical gun, the exact model of Frank's.

When Frank put down his gun to climb through the fence, Al grabbed him in the wire, shoved his own gun into position, and fired. Then, all that was needed was a quick tangle around the stick and trigger guard, a touch of Frank's hand on the stock for fingerprints, then a moment for Al to pick up Frank's gun as if it were his and run to the Jeep."

They had started along a dark road, and Elaine shuddered, turning to look at Bruce's strong profile, illuminated by the dash light. "If the guns are just alike," she said, "that's going to be hard to prove."

Bruce shook his head. "Those guns are custom-made, and each one has an identifying number engraved on it in an inconspicuous spot. Al thought, and rightly, that neither Hanley nor his deputies would know that, so he wasn't worried at first. He took Frank's gun back to the house and put it in the gun cabinet, and planned to ask for 'Frank's gun' after the inquest, pretending he wanted to return it. He didn't know you were going to move into the house the next day. He must have had a few nervous moments over that, but it still worked out, or at least he thought it did. He got his own gun back later with the same story of returning it and got away with it — until I asked Hanley what day he 'returned' it and found out it was the first day of the storm." Bruce looked over at Elaine and smiled. "I knew that wasn't true, and I told Hanley Frank's gun had been in the cabinet all along. That started Hanley looking, and he's a bulldog. He was a big help. His men had found the identifying number on the murder weapon and had written it down, along with all the other data on fingerprints and so forth. But they hadn't thought to check on it — they thought it was a personal number Jeffrey put on it in case of theft. Townsend told them where to check and they called Fortner's and found out it was Al's gun they'd had."

Elaine sighed. "That's proof, then — unless Al claims there was some mix-up and the deputy picked up the wrong gun."

Bruce laughed grimly. "He'll probably try just that. But it won't work. Hanley's smart — he asked if we'd bring Frank's gun down for fingerprinting, and we did. They found both Frank's and Al's prints on it, but that was all. Al's gun had Furman's prints all over it."

"That's right," Elaine agreed excitedly. "Furman only touched the gun tangled in the wire! Such a little thing."

"Big enough," Bruce said. "Al will throw himself on the mercy of the court when he hears that. And he'll probably get a light sentence. Juries are kind to wronged husbands who kill their wives' lovers."

"Beth was Frank's way out, I guess."

"Yes. Frank had boasted to the men at the hunt club that Beth Fenton was going to be his ticket back to the good life. Beth and the Harrison millions. It was probably that gossip that got back to Al." Bruce frowned. "I'm a little sorry for Beth. She was crazy about Frank, head over heels. It's pathetic, the way she hangs on to that car. Her only memento."

Elaine was silent. To her mind, Beth was lucky. She would soon have been disillusioned with Frank. The whole thing seemed typical of the worst traits of Frank's crowd: the immorality and selfishness, dishonesty and greed. And now murder. How had she ever thought Bruce would be like them? She looked over at him and caught him glancing at her.

"Long thoughts, angel? Do you realize that Al *had* gotten away with it, until you came on the scene with your note and your guilt?" He smiled at her startled look. She hadn't thought of that. "By the way, how are those guilt feelings now?"

"Gone," Elaine said thoughtfully, "completely gone. I thought I'd gotten over it weeks ago, but I think I must have buried it instead. Tonight, when I found out the truth, it was as though a stone had been lifted away. I'll never be able to thank you enough."

"You don't have to," Bruce said gruffly. "I've learned quite a bit myself."

Elaine settled back, looking ahead. It seemed to be taking quite a long time to get back to Farley's, even though the big complex was outside of town limits. The road ahead looked familiar . . . winding upward. Oh, no! How could she tell him now that she never wanted to see his beloved house again? She steeled herself and turned toward him.

"Bruce, please — take me back to the motel."

He knew, even if she hadn't mentioned the house. "We aren't going to stay up here," he said quietly, "but I want to take you there, just for a while. All right?"

"All right." She looked away, knowing she couldn't refuse him anything now. Maybe she'd never be able to refuse him again, unless he asked her to live in that house.

Staring out at the side of the mountain, she tried to think back and discover when it was that she had begun to feel that way. Maybe the day they had discovered the dingy gun in the cabinet. Or the night, perhaps, when Al had been there and there had been such a scene. Or maybe the first time Bruce had gone away and she had realized that she loved him, that he loved the house, and that if they stayed together . . . She shook her head and went back to watching the road. Whatever or whenever, the aura in the house had gradually grown stronger. It had reeked of the life she didn't want to live. Frank's house. She could no longer think of it any other way.

Yet it wasn't that bad, after all, going in. Bruce's arm was around her as they entered, and in the fireplace there were still a few dark red coals. Elaine stood watching Bruce as he built up the fire again, skillfully laying on the bit of kindling and then the logs. When it was burning brightly, he went into the kitchen and came out with thick roast beef sandwiches and a bottle of wine.

Elaine smiled, remembering the night when the power was off and they'd built their 'cave' around this same fireplace. She had left her heavy coat on the rack in the foyer; now she took off her suit jacket and flung it into a chair. Sitting down on the soft hearth rug in front of the fire, she reached for a sandwich.

Bruce grinned and sat down with her on the rug, looking completely familiar in the red-and-black-plaid shirt. Elaine laughed, her face suddenly merry, her eyes sparkling.

"I remember you," she said, "when you had only one shirt and one pair of jeans.

You almost wore out the washer and dryer."

Bruce chuckled, wolfing down his sandwich. "I was poor but proud in those days." He poured the wine into two glasses and gave her one. "Besides, there was this beautiful woman around, and I was trying to make an impression."

She giggled, finishing her sandwich. "You did very well." She took her wineglass and leaned back, propping herself on the bottom of one of the big chairs, dreamily looking into the fire as she drank the wine. The sense of release and the new freedom she felt were beginning to sink in; the last tatter of worry had floated away. She seemed to be floating herself, light and relaxed. She turned her head slightly and watched the firelight flicker on Bruce's strong face, putting gleams of dark red in the black beard, and another flicker of flame that had nothing to do with the fireplace began to pool invitingly deep inside her. She went on looking at him while she finished the wine, her eyes following the lines of the broad back that tapered down to lean hips, then traveling the long, muscled strength of his legs.

Bruce seemed lost in reverie, watching the fire and the black logs falling in a shower of glowing coals, his face relaxed and thoughtful. Elaine was lost, too, in a memory of the first time they had made love — here, in front of the fire. The warmth inside her grew, flowing through her veins and tightening her rounded breasts, tipping them with heat. But still Bruce sat staring at the fire as if he were alone.

Well, she couldn't *ask* him! Maybe he didn't feel like making love. She lounged there thinking of various ways to capture his interest, but mostly they seemed too blatant. Finally, she kicked off her shoes and sat up, drawing her feet around to one side, making a lap of her straight skirt. Then, methodically, she began taking down her hair, dropping the big tortoiseshell pins in her lap.

Bruce had turned to her as he heard her move, and now, with his arms resting lightly on his upraised knees, he watched and remembered the first night in this house, when Elaine had worn that same silk blouse with a long forest-green skirt.

She had sat in the chair that was behind her now, and taken down her slipping knot of hair to put it up again. His reaction then had been powerful, and now, knowing the passion in that slender, small body, it was even stronger. The way the silk of the blouse smoothed tightly up from her supple waist and swelled over her breasts made the palms of his hands burn. Her skirt had hiked up over her knees, exposing the tender beginning of her thighs, and the sudden memory of those thighs wrapped around him and her fierce whisper of '*Now!*' made his already heated loins ache. But was it too soon? Was she still thinking of that meeting, of tension and lies, cheating and killing? He watched the rich mahogany hair tumble down her back, saw her slim hands come up lazily and sweep it back, and then the fine-boned face turned toward him and he saw the dark silver eyes, the sensuously seductive smile.

He moved fast, dragging her across the space between them with one long arm, easing her down on the soft rug, covering her, holding her there with his weight. His hands groped in the silken mass of hair and held her head between his palms, covering her face with wild kisses. "Don't look at me like that," he said hoarsely, "unless you mean it. I'm starving for you."

She struggled to get her breath. "I mean it!" she gasped. "Oh, how I mean it!"

Bruce laughed shakily and sat up, pulling her with him, anchoring her against him with his strong thighs while his hand ran over her feverishly, remembering, memorizing. He unbuttoned her blouse, pushed aside her bra, groaned at the feeling of her bare breasts in his palm, then bent her over one arm and lowered his mouth to the quivering nipples.

Elaine made sounds, urgent small growls she hardly recognized as her own. She was pressed tightly against his bulging loins; she could feel the seductive heat against her and her own loins responded with a wrenching desire, a flaming need. When his big hand slid up under her skirt and caressed her inner thighs, her body rippled and swung, begging for more.

Panting, she dragged his head away from her breasts and fastened her open mouth on his, her tongue flicking, coaxing.

Suddenly, she felt his hard-held control go, his body surge, his strength centered full force on what they both wanted. Somehow her blouse was gone, her panty hose was off; in some manner, his shirt had disappeared from his massive chest, his jeans were pushed down, but still clothes dangled from them as they came together in an explosive rush, an impassioned, awkward scramble on the rug that ended in a deep, triumphant sigh, a small, satisfied moan.

Locked together, eyes closed in contentment, they moved, slowly but surely making the few, sinuous motions it took to hurtle them over a crumbling barrier into the thrumming beat of sexual ecstasy. Panting, they made tiny surges that sent echoes of pleasure following the fading beat, until, at last satisfied, they lay together quietly.

Elaine waited until her heartbeat slowed to near normal before she opened her eyes. Looking to the side, she could see the top of Bruce's head, a thick wisp of hair that stood up and glistened in the firelight. She stroked it down with a lazy hand, feeling his bearded face move slightly against her neck, after which his mouth opened and sucked in a bit of tender flesh. She could also feel her skirt, now no more than a wrinkled bundle around her upper hips, and her bra, pushed up above her breasts and twisted.

She sighed, her hands running over his bare, muscled back. "It might have been better," she said, "if we'd undressed first."

"I don't see how it could have been better," Bruce answered, raising his head to look at her. "But we can try it that way next time." He looked supremely contented, his brown eyes velvety again, his grin brilliant. He leaned, kissing her eyes, the end of her nose, her mouth, light and tender. Then he eased away, taking his weight from her. "Stylish," he added, looking her over. "You should wear your bra that way more often. It's very becoming."

"I like your jeans, too," Elaine said appreciatively, gazing at the thick bundle that covered his lower legs and feet. "You look like a merman. Why didn't you kick them off?"

Bruce stared down his length morosely. "Boots," he said. "There are boots under there. I'm not sure I can stand up."

Elaine broke into laughter she couldn't subdue. Hastily gathering up her scattered clothes, she kept erupting again in giggles as Bruce fought with the tangle of jeans and laced boots.

Even in the bath upstairs, trying to get her clothing in order and her hair back up, she exploded again in laughter, thinking of the crazy scene. It had been so funny, yet she was still awed by the passion that had flared between them after being apart. Her mood gentled, a dream began, a shining vista of a future stretched before her. The two of them, in Atlanta. New beginnings that could now ignore the past. She went back down the stairs lightly, slightly wrinkled but none the worse for wear, and found Bruce coming out of the kitchen, properly dressed and carrying a pot of coffee and two cups.

"I thought we were going back to the

motel," she said warily. "Isn't that what you said?"

"We are," he answered, putting the cups and pot on the table between the two chairs, "but first coffee and talk."

Reassured, Elaine sank into the chair she had always used and watched his deft hands pour the coffee into the fragile cups. For some reason, it reminded her of the only time she had ever seen him make an awkward, uncoordinated movement. She could still see him grabbing up that broken wineglass, crunching it in his hand, turning it over. The still-pink line of a deep scar made her wince.

Following her gaze, Bruce closed his hand over her fingers, bent, and kissed her own palm before he let go. "That scar is very useful," he said with a faint smile. "It's a handy reminder of my monumental stupidity. I think — at least I hope — I learned something from that scene."

"I hope we both did," Elaine answered. "I could have told you I wasn't ready for marriage without making all those crazy accusations. I don't know what was the matter with me."

"I think I do," Bruce said, settling into his chair. He raised his cup and drank, looking at her over the rim with his brown eyes quizzical. "And I've done something about it." He set the cup down, smiling again. "I brought you here tonight for the last time, angel. Maybe because this is the place we started, maybe just to relive some good memories while we can. It's the last time for me, too. I've sold it."

Elaine jerked up, coffee spilling over the rim of her cup, pooling in the saucer. "Oh, Bruce! You love this house!"

He shook his head. "I don't love this house, Elaine. I love *you*. The house is nice, but it's not worth one day of being alone and wondering where you are and what you're doing. I guess it took that quarrel to make me realize what I had been doing to you. When I cooled off enough to think about what you had said, I felt stupid as hell."

He sat forward, looking again at the fire. "If I'd given it a few moments' thought, I would have known before, but I was too wrapped up in that investigation. Anyway, the investigation taught me what kind of man Jeffrey was. I hadn't known before, I'd barely met him, but I realized that *you* knew, and that the thought of living in the house he built and maybe having a similar life was just impossible for you to consider. And you were so raw inside with shame and guilt for letting the bastard down that it just made it worse." He glanced around at her and smiled faintly. "That wouldn't have bothered any other woman I know, angel. At times you're too idealistic."

Elaine's head was bent. "I know. But it wasn't just that. Frank never treated me cruelly; he was more than generous. And he never understood why I resented his affairs — everyone had affairs in that crowd. He couldn't see anything wrong with the life we led, either. I hurt him — as much as anyone could hurt him — when I left. And, I felt shame. I had told myself I should stick it out because I'd made those vows, but in the end I couldn't." She looked up at Bruce. "I knew there had to be more to living than that. But the charge of desertion was right, Bruce, I did desert him."

"You deserted that kind of life," Bruce

answered grimly. "And then I came along and kept you in Frank's house, along with Frank's guns and possessions, dragged you through scenes with the Fentons and then left you alone half the time without telling you my suspicions or even hinting at what I was doing. Then, I really got brilliant. I tried to push you into a marriage that would keep you in the same situation. Any fool should have known that what was to me just a new, beautiful house was to you a constant reminder of everything you hated."

Elaine stared at him in awe. "I was right to refuse," she said weakly. "No woman ought to be married to a man who understands her that well."

Bruce laughed and leaned back. "Maybe, but you're going to be, just as soon as I can talk you into it. If you want to try your wings in Atlanta, that's great. We'll live there if you want. Or anywhere else. My only requirement is that we live together."

She put down her coffee cup, stood up, and moved to her rightful place, curling into his lap, relaxing luxuriously as his arms went around her. Maybe she'd never understand him that well, but she did know it was a wrench for him to give up his mountains. "What if I said I'd like a place here?" she asked softly.

Bruce kissed her, his tongue making sensuous promises. "I wasn't going to mention it yet, but I own that hillside where my parents lived, and part of the valley. Might make a nice place for a summer home."

She sighed, trying hard to sound disgusted and failing miserably, due to her smile. "I should have known. You never give up."

"Not when I really want something." He nuzzled her neck, breathing in her feminine fragrance. Her soft warmth in his lap was becoming irresistibly tantalizing, reminding him vividly of that wide expanse of bed he had seen in the room at Farley's. Surfacing, he looked at his watch. "Let's go, angel. It's late, and we'll be getting up early."

"We're going to the motel?" She had begun to resign herself to staying here, knowing it wouldn't be long.

His thick brows rose. "Naturally. After

all, this isn't my house, I just borrowed if for the evening. The new owners move in tomorrow."

"But your clothes!"

He stood up, lifting her with him, and sighed. "You never looked in the back of the wagon. It's as full as your trunk. *We're* moving, angel, together."

That had a fine sound. She stood looking at him for a moment, then laughed and hugged him, feeling wonderful.

"You had it all planned. Such confidence. Are you really that sure of me?"

"Almost," he said, pulling her toward the foyer, "but not quite. For instance, I'm not sure when you'll give in and marry me."

She took his mackinaw from the rack and held it for him, pushing it up over his wide shoulders. "How about Monday? That's New Year's, isn't it?"

He turned and picked her up, staring into her eyes. "You mean it," he said softly, and put her down, grabbing her coat and pushing her arms into it. "Hurry up! We've got to get to that motel."

"Listen," she said breathlessly, half

running as he pulled her through the door and down the steps. "This time . . . "

"We will," he said, without slackening his pace. "We'll take everything off, slowly."

He hadn't waited for the suggestion, but, then, he always understood her.

THE END

Other titles in the
Ulverscroft Large Print Series:

TO FIGHT THE WILD
Rod Ansell and Rachel Percy

Lost in uncharted Australian bush, Rod Ansell survived by hunting and trapping wild animals, improvising shelter and using all the bushman's skills he knew.

COROMANDEL
Pat Barr

India in the 1830s is a hot, uncomfortable place, where the East India Company still rules. Amelia and her new husband find themselves caught up in the animosities which seethe between the old order and the new.

THE SMALL PARTY
Lillian Beckwith

A frightening journey to safety begins for Ruth and her small party as their island is caught up in the dangers of armed insurrection.

NURSE ALICE IN LOVE
Theresa Charles

Accepting the post of nurse to little Fernie Sherrod, Alice Everton could not guess at the romance, suspense and danger which lay ahead at the Sherrod's isolated estate.

POIROT INVESTIGATES
Agatha Christie

Two things bind these eleven stories together — the brilliance and uncanny skill of the diminutive Belgian detective, and the stupidity of his Watson-like partner, Captain Hastings.

LET LOOSE THE TIGERS
Josephine Cox

Queenie promised to find the long-lost son of the frail, elderly murderess, Hannah Jason. But her enquiries threatened to unlock the cage where crucial secrets had long been held captive.

TIGER TIGER
Frank Ryan

A young man involved in drugs is found murdered. This is the first event which will draw Detective Inspector Sandy Woodings into a whirlpool of murder and deceit.

CAROLINE MINUSCULE
Andrew Taylor

Caroline Minuscule, a medieval script, is the first clue to the whereabouts of a cache of diamonds. The search becomes a deadly kind of fairy story in which several murders have an other-worldly quality.

LONG CHAIN OF DEATH
Sarah Wolf

During the Second World War four American teenagers from the same town join the Army together. Forty-two years later, the son of one of the soldiers realises that someone is systematically wiping out the families of the four men.

THE LISTERDALE MYSTERY
Agatha Christie

Twelve short stories ranging from the light-hearted to the macabre, diverse mysteries ingeniously and plausibly contrived and convincingly unravelled.

TO BE LOVED
Lynne Collins

Andrew married the woman he had always loved despite the knowledge that Sarah married him for reasons of her own. So much heartache could have been avoided if only he had known how vital it was to be loved.

ACCUSED NURSE
Jane Converse

Paula found herself accused of a crime which could cost her her job, her nurse's reputation, and even the man she loved, unless the truth came to light.

THE PLEASURES OF AGE
Robert Morley

The author, British stage and screen star, now eighty, is enjoying the pleasures of age. He has drawn on his experiences to write this witty, entertaining and informative book.

THE VINEGAR SEED
Maureen Peters

The first book in a trilogy which follows the exploits of two sisters who leave Ireland in 1861 to seek their fortune in England.

A VERY PAROCHIAL MURDER
John Wainwright

A mugging in the genteel seaside town turned to murder when the victim died. Then the body of a young tearaway is washed ashore and Detective Inspector Lyle is determined that a second killing will not go unpunished.

DEATH ON A HOT SUMMER NIGHT
Anne Infante

Micky Douglas is either accident-prone or someone is trying to kill him. He finds himself caught in a desperate race to save his ex-wife and others from a ruthless gang.

HOLD DOWN A SHADOW
Geoffrey Jenkins

Maluti Rider, with the help of four of the world's most wanted men, is determined to destroy the Katse Dam and release a killer flood.

THAT NICE MISS SMITH
Nigel Morland

A reconstruction and reassessment of the trial in 1857 of Madeleine Smith, who was acquitted by a verdict of Not Proven of poisoning her lover, Emile L'Angelier.

SEASONS OF MY LIFE
Hannah Hauxwell
and Barry Cockcroft

The story of Hannah Hauxwell's struggle to survive on a desolate farm in the Yorkshire Dales with little money, no electricity and no running water.

TAKING OVER
Shirley Lowe and Angela Ince

A witty insight into what happens when women take over in the boardroom and their husbands take over chores, children and chickenpox.

AFTER MIDNIGHT STORIES,
The Fourth Book Of

A collection of sixteen of the best of today's ghost stories, all different in style and approach but all combining to give the reader that special midnight shiver.

DEATH TRAIN
Robert Byrne

The tale of a freight train out of control and leaking a paralytic nerve gas that turns America's West into a scene of chemical catastrophe in which whole towns are rendered helpless.

THE ADVENTURE
OF THE
CHRISTMAS PUDDING
Agatha Christie

In the introduction to this short story collection the author wrote "This book of Christmas fare may be described as 'The Chef's Selection'. I am the Chef!"

RETURN TO BALANDRA
Grace Driver

Returning to her Caribbean island home, Suzanne looks forward to being with her parents again, but most of all she longs to see Wim van Branden, a coffee planter she has known all her life.

SKINWALKERS
Tony Hillerman

The peace of the land between the sacred mountains is shattered by three murders. Is a 'skinwalker', one who has rejected the harmony of the Navajo way, the murderer?

A PARTICULAR PLACE
Mary Hocking

How is Michael Hoath, newly arrived vicar of St. Hilary's, to meet the demands of his flock and his strained marriage? Further complications follow when he falls hopelessly in love with a married parishioner.

A MATTER OF MISCHIEF
Evelyn Hood

A saga of the weaving folk in 18th century Scotland. Physician Gavin Knox was desperately seeking a cure for the pox that ravaged the slums of Glasgow and Paisley, but his adored wife, Margaret, stood in the way.

DEAD SPIT
Janet Edmonds

Government vet Linus Rintoul attempts to solve a mystery which plunges him into the esoteric world of pedigree dogs, murder and terrorism, and Crufts Dog Show proves to be far more exciting than he had bargained for . . .

A BARROW IN THE BROADWAY
Pamela Evans

Adopted by the Gordillo family, Rosie Goodson watched their business grow from a street barrow to a chain of supermarkets. But passion, bitterness and her unhappy marriage aliented her from them.

THE GOLD AND THE DROSS
Eleanor Farnes

Lorna found it hard to make ends meet for herself and her mother and then by chance she met two men — one a famous author and one a rich banker. But could she really expect to be happy with either man?

THE SONG OF THE PINES
Christina Green

Taken to a Greek island as substitute for David Nicholas's secretary, Annie quickly falls prey to the island's charms and to the charms of both Marcus, the Greek, and David himself.

GOODBYE DOCTOR GARLAND
Marjorie Harte

The story of a woman doctor who gave too much to her profession and almost lost her personal happiness.

DIGBY
Pamela Hill

Welcomed at courts throughout Europe, Kenelm Digby was the particular favourite of the Queen of France, who wanted him to be her lover, but the beautiful Venetia was the mainspring of his life.

PREJUDICED WITNESS
Dilys Gater

Fleur Rowley finds when she leaves London for her 'author's retreat' in the wilds of North Wales that she is drawn, in spite of herself, into an old tragedy.

GENTLE TYRANT
Lucy Gillen

Working as Ross McAdam's secretary, Laura couldn't imagine why his bitchy ex-wife should see her as a rival.

DEAR CAPRICE
Juliet Gray

Clifford Fortune married Caprice but his brother, Luke, knew the marriage was a mistake. He could allow himself to love Caprice blindly but that would be betraying his own brother.

IN PALE BATTALIONS
Robert Goddard

Leonora Galloway has waited all her life to learn the truth about her father, slain on the Somme before she was born, the truth about the death of her mother and the mystery of an unsolved wartime murder.

A DREAM FOR TOMORROW
Grace Goodwin

In her new position as resident nurse at Coombe Magna, Karen Stevens has to bear the emnity of the beautiful Lisa, secretary to the doctor-on-call.

AFTER EMMA
Sheila Hocken

Following the author's previous auto-biographies — EMMA & I, and EMMA & Co., she relates more of the hilarious (and sometimes despairing) antics of her guide dogs.

LEAVE IT TO THE HANGMAN
Bill Knox

Dope, dynamite, guns, currency — whatever it was John Kilburn and his son Pat had known how to get it in or out of England, if the price was right. But their luck changed when one of them killed a cop.

A VIOLENT END
Emma Page

To Chief Inspector Kelsey there was no shortage of suspects when Karen Boland was murdered, and that was before he discovered that she stood to inherit substantially at twenty-one.

SILENCE IN HANOVER CLOSE
Anne Perry

In 1884 Robert York is found brutally murdered at his home in Hanover Close. When, three years later, Inspector Pitt is asked to investigate, the murder remains unsolved.

A RARE BENEDICTINE
Ellis Peters

Three vintage tales of medieval intrigue and treachery featuring the author's monastic sleuth Brother Cadfael.

POIROT'S EARLY CASES
Agatha Christie

In this collection of eighteen stories, Hercule Poirot begins his celebrated career in crime.

THE SILVER LINK
— THE SILKEN LIE
Lynn Granger

Elspeth is determined to preserve her Scottish heritage and the Elliot name, but running Everanlea, a large hill farm, presents problems.